The Girls They Left Behind

Bernice Thurman Hunter

Fitzhenry & Whiteside

Published in Canada by Fitzhenry & Whiteside, 195 Allstate Parkway, Markham, Ontario L3R 4T8

Published in the United States by Fitzhenry & Whiteside, 121 Harvard Avenue, Suite 2, Allston, Massachusetts 02134

www.fitzhenry.ca   **godwit@fitzhenry.ca**

10 9 8 7 6 5 4 3 2 1

Library and Archives Canada Cataloguing in Publication

Hunter, Bernice Thurman
    The girls they left behind / Bernice Thurman Hunter.

ISBN 1-55041-927-7

    1. World War, 1939-1945—Canada—Juvenile fiction. I. Title.

PS8565.U577G57 2005   jC813'.54   C2004-906815-6

U.S. Publisher Cataloging-in-Publication Data
(Library of Congress Standards)

Hunter, Bernice Thurman.
    The girls they left behind / Bernice Thurman Hunter.
[192] p. : cm.
Summary: During World War II, a spunky teenager finds a way to contribute to the war effort while she waits for the boys in her life to come home.
ISBN 1-55041-927-7 (pbk.)
1. World War, 1939-1945 _ Fiction. I. Title.
[Fic] 22 PS3570.H87 2005

Fitzhenry & Whiteside acknowledges with thanks the Canada Council for the Arts, the Government of Canada through the Book Publishing Industry Development Program (BPIDP), and the Ontario Arts Council for their support of our publishing program.

Design by Fortunato Design Inc.

Cover images: Image of girl: Harry Rowed / National Film Board of Canada. Photothèque / Library and Archives Canada / PA-112824.
Image of pilot: Photo of Sgt. A. Gourd appears with permission on the Society of Bomber Command Historians Website. Repeated attempts were made without success to contact the family of Sgt. Gourd for their extended permission.

Printed and bound in Canada

The Girls
They Left Behind

Chapter 1

Dear Diary:

This is my very first diary. I have never kept a diary before, but since Eloise Wilkinson gave it to me for a bridesmaid's gift, I thought I should start it with her wedding.

Eloise is my best friend and she got married to her boyfriend, Private James Foster, today. Jim had come home on embarkation leave and asked Eloise to marry him before he went overseas. Well, Eloise is only eighteen years old (one year older than I am, almost to the day), so she had to have her father's signature on a permission-to-marry form. Her mother said she wouldn't sign such a thing, but mothers can't sign anyway unless the father is dead. So all Mrs. Wilkinson could do was cry her eyes out through the whole ceremony. I don't know why she was crying because Jim is nice (homely, but nice) and Eloise looked lovely in her white chiffon wedding dress and pillbox hat with a veil. I could see her big dark eyes shining right through the white netting. Eloise and I are opposites. She has wavy blonde hair and brown eyes; I have straight black hair and blue eyes. She carried a bouquet of June flowers that my mother picked out of our garden. I wore my Easter dress which, luckily, I had only worn once so it is practically new. It's sky blue but a little darker, trimmed with white eyelet. I bobby-pinned white carnations on either side of my head just above my ears and I wore blue and white spectator pumps. The only problem was—no stockings. Eloise had none either, so we painted our legs with bronze leg-do and then we drew a perfect line up the back of each other's legs so no one could tell that we weren't wearing real stockings.

It was a small wedding in the minister's parlour. Eloise didn't have time to send out invitations because Jim's proposal was so sudden that only family and close friends could be invited. After the wedding we went back to the Wilkinson's house. Mrs. Wilkinson's friend, Mrs. Penrose, served tea and fancy sandwiches and wedding cake, and we toasted the bride with Canada Dry Ginger Ale in cornflower crystal glasses. Then Jim and Eloise went off on a two-day honeymoon trip in Jim's brother's Chevrolet Coupe. (coo-pay!)

Everything would have gone off without a hitch (pardon the pun) except that two of Eloise's boy cousins smeared Just Married with soap all over the windows of the Chevrolet Coupe and tied tin cans to the back bumper. Well, Jim's brother, the car's rightful owner, got furious and went roaring up the street after them shaking his fist. This started Mrs. Wilkinson crying again. Mr. Wilkinson said the noise of the yelling and the tin cans bouncing up the road was enough to waken the dead. Then he put his arm around Mrs. Wilkinson's shoulders and I heard him say, "Never mind, Mother, you've still got me," as he led her back into the house, which made her cry all the harder.

It is supposed to be a secret, where the bride and groom go on their honeymoon. But Eloise told me because I am her best friend and bridesmaid. They went to Niagara Falls, which is about a hundred miles away. I've never been to Niagara Falls myself. I've seen pictures though, on Aunt Marie's stereoscope. It looks beautiful and if I ever have a honeymoon I'd like to go there.

I hope Eloise and Jim are having a good time on their honeymoon. What a lovely word…honeymoon.

P.S. I love this little book. It's blue leatherette and my name is embossed in gold leaf on the cover. I'm going to try to write in it every day.

Signed,
Natalie.

P.S. Natalie is my pen name. My real name is not fit to print.

Chapter 2

The next Saturday

"Beryl!" My mother's high-pitched voice came sailing up the stairs. "Somebody wants you on the telephone!"

Oh, how I hated that name! There ought to be a law that says you can pick your own name when you reach your teens, I thought as I ran down to get the phone.

It was my boyfriend, Will Ashby, on the line. He lives up the street. We have been going steady now for three weeks.

"How's about the show tonight?" Will asked.

"What's on?"

"I dunno. Let's go find out."

"Okay," I agreed.

"I'll call for you after supper," he said.

"Okay," I said and hung up.

My mother had been listening to my half of the conversation. "What time will you be home?" she asked.

"Oh, really, Mother." I gave her a disgruntled frown. "I'm seventeen!" Then I went upstairs to decide what to wear.

We walked along College Street holding hands. The movie

at the College Show was *Mrs. Miniver*, starring Greer Garson. It was a romantic war story. But the newsreel, "The Eyes and Ears of the World," showed just how unromantic war really was—bombed buildings in London and King George himself standing among the rubble, talking to his people like an ordinary man. Then terrible scenes of dead soldiers on battlefields and ships burning at sea and corpses washed up on the beaches, some floating face down in the water, their steel helmets still on their heads. I had to hide my eyes.

"I hope it lasts till December fifth," Will said in an excited whisper. I knew what he meant. December fifth was Will's eighteenth birthday, so he'd be able to join up without his parents' consent.

I wondered if he'd ask me to marry him before he went to war like Jim had asked Eloise. Eloise had confided in me that the reason she was so anxious to get married was that, if you didn't marry your boyfriend before he went overseas, some English girl would nab him for sure.

I glanced sideways at Will. He was staring, fascinated, at the carnage on the screen. Even if he does ask me, I thought, my father would never sign that paper. Besides, I wasn't that crazy about Will Ashby. For one thing, his top teeth stuck out (they were sticking out right then, wet and shiny, in the flickering light of the screen). Seeing them reminded me of our first kiss in the Lansdowne Theatre on our first date. Our teeth had clashed together and he had burst out laughing. I didn't think it was funny. And I hated his laugh, too. "HeeeHawww! HeeeHawww!" He brayed just like a donkey.

Besides, I knew what a kiss should feel like. I had kissed lots of boys goodbye at Union Station, and by comparison Will's kiss failed miserably.

Chapter 3

Summer, 1943

I was glad when the school year ended. I had one more year to go to get my commercial diploma. But right now all I was interested in was finding a summer job. My friend, Myra Adams, who was in the same form as me at Bloor Collegiate, had read in the newspaper that Eatons Department Store was advertising for help. So we decided to go downtown together and apply.

"Wear your navy skirt and white blouse," my mother advised, "and not too much lipstick if you want to make a good impression."

Myra's mother must have given her the same advice, because she had no lipstick on at all. But as soon as we got settled on the circular wooden seat at the back of the Dundas Streetcar, out came our lipsticks and compacts and we started dolling up our faces.

After asking a saleslady and a floorwalker in the Main Store where the employment office was, we finally found it on Albert Street. There were about a dozen girls there already. No boys.

A severe-looking woman, wearing rimless glasses on a

chain, handed us application forms. Myra and I sat side by side at a long, wooden, ink-stained table and started filling them out. Halfway down the page I asked Myra, "What are you putting down for job preference?"

She glanced over at my application. "Your name's not Natalie," she whispered.

"It is now," I said.

"I don't think you'll get away with it," Myra frowned. "Why don't you put your real name down? I did."

"Well, at least your name is interesting," I said. "What did you put for job preference?"

"Office worker," Myra said. "I got good marks in typing and shorthand. What did you put?"

"Candy counter." I had almost failed shorthand.

"Why on earth would you want to count candies?" Myra asked, squinching her nose.

"Don't be dumb. I mean I'd like to work at the candy counter where they sell Cottage Sweets. I like talking to people. And I love the smell of chocolate."

"Ohhh!" Myra said.

On our way home—we lived across the street from each other on Gladstone Avenue just south of College Street— we stopped at Loblaws Groceteria to do some shopping for our mothers.

"Can you trade me some butter coupons for sugar coupons, Beryl?" Myra asked.

"Why don't you ask Natalie?" I suggested.

"Okay, I'll try, but I don't think I'll ever get used to it."

"Well, try."

"Natalie, can you trade me butter coupons for sugar coupons?"

"Sure," I grinned. Natalie sounded so sophisticated compared to Beryl. "My mother always needs extra sugar for her baking."

"Well, my dad won't eat oleomargarine. When it's on the table he says, 'Pass the grease,' and makes my mother mad."

"Come on down the back," I said.

The canned-goods aisle at the very back of the store was empty of shoppers. So we surreptitiously traded ration coupons. You have to be careful because it's against the law to trade coupons. You could get fined if you get caught. My uncle by marriage, Duncan Filmore, got caught red-handed trading gasoline coupons for beer coupons and was fined ten dollars. My Aunt Hope, Dad's sister (Uncle Duncan calls her Hopeless), got mad as hops and wouldn't speak to him for weeks (which he said was fine by him).

After supper we went to the show and saw *Waterloo Bridge* starring Robert Taylor and Vivien Leigh. Eloise Wilkinson (Foster now, I keep forgetting) went with us and she talked through the whole movie.

"I think my hubby is even handsomer than Robert Taylor, don't you?" she whispered to me. Eloise never said "Jim" or "my husband." It was always "my hubby," which I found particularly annoying.

I pretended not to hear—picturing Jim in my mind, what could I say?

During an amorous love scene, Eloise held up her left hand and wiggled her fingers so that the tiny diamond in her engagement ring caught a sparkle in the projection light. "I know *exactly* how she feels," she sighed breathlessly.

She was always doing that now, implying that she knew something we didn't know. I decided I liked her better before she got married.

Eloise kept up the whispering all through the movie until Myra leaned over and told her to shut up. Then they didn't speak to each other for the rest of the night.

"Have we got any shampoo?" I asked my mother when I got home.

"Oh, Beryl, you know you can't buy shampoo for love nor money now," my mother reminded me. "You'll just have to melt some Sunlight."

So I shaved some of the yellow brick soap into a pot of boiling water, stirred it until it melted, and then when it cooled down enough so I could stand it, I washed my hair and gave it three vinegar rinses. (Sunlight sticks like glue.) Then I did it up in pincurls and wrapped it in a toilet-paper turban. Next I painted my legs with Eatonia brand leg-do called "Velva Film." The salesgirl at Eatons said it was guaranteed not to rub off. If it did, you could bring back the bottle and get your money back, she said. That's the way it was with all Eatons' merchandise: Goods Satisfactory or Money Refunded. Timothy Eaton, the store's founder, was the first merchant in Toronto to ever give such an incredible guarantee. And it must have worked because Eatons was the most famous and I dare say, successful, department store in Canada. At least in Toronto.

I sure hoped the salesgirl was right about it not rubbing off. My mother would have a fit if she found brown smears on her white bed sheets.

I'll try to make one application last three days, I thought, replacing the cap. It's so darned expensive! Twenty-five cents a bottle.

Chapter 4

Dear Diary:

This is the saddest day of my life so far. My favourite cousin, Carmen Baker, left for overseas tonight. Carmen is my second cousin once removed because his mother, Aunt Marie, is really my mother's aunt but they are almost the same age. Anyway I've always called her "aunt" and my mother has always called her "Marie." They grew up together like sisters.

I can't believe Carmen is old enough to go, but he is. He turned eighteen in May so he didn't need his parents' consent to join up. In his case the parent is Aunt Marie because Uncle Harley ran off when Carmen was only two years old and has never been seen since. (Well, somebody thought they saw him, once, preaching on a soapbox at Yonge and Queen Streets, but it turned out to be a case of mistaken identity.) Anyway, I think it's ridiculous that you can't vote or get married until you're twenty-one, but you can go to war and maybe get yourself killed when you're only eighteen.

Poor Aunt Marie—she was so upset she couldn't

bear to go to Union Station to see him off. Carmen is her only child. (His twin brother, Cary, died at birth.) My mother says it is a tragedy to have an only child because if you lose him or her you never get over it. Her cousin Violet had an only child, a girl named June, who drowned at the mouth of the Humber River more than twenty years ago, and Violet is still in mourning. Every year on little June's birthday, Violet holds her blonde curl—cut off and given to her by the undertaker—in the palm of her hand, and tears stream down her face and drip off her chin, soaking the curl. Then she lets it dry on a tea towel and puts it back in the little blue jewellery box she keeps it in (she says it is more precious than any jewel) until little June's next birthday. I was an only child myself until I was seven, and then along came Richard and spoiled everything.

Carmen is so excited about being a gunner in the RCAF that his excitement is contagious. And he looks marvellous in his airforce uniform. It has transformed him from a shy, self-conscious boy to a dashing, handsome hero. All my girlfriends (except Eloise, of course) are in love with him. To tell the truth, if he wasn't my flesh-and-blood cousin (once removed), I think I'd be in love with him myself.

Five of us went down to Union Station to see him off. I was the last person to kiss him goodbye. I was crying so hard that I couldn't speak, so I never did tell him how proud I was of him or how much I loved him. "Don't cry, kiddo," he whispered in my ear. "I'll be back just as soon as I've bombed 'Jerry' right off the map." Then he was swept away in a laughing, roaring tide of airforce blue.

As the train began to move he managed to squeeze his head and arm out the window. He yelled something I couldn't hear and waved with his wedge cap. Suddenly the cap flew out of his hand and bounced along the platform. I ran and grabbed it up before it got trampled by hundreds of feet or kicked under the huge steel wheels. Then I waved it back at him as the train steamed out of the station.

I hope he's got another cap because I am going to keep this one. It's hanging on the clothes hook inside my bedroom door until he comes home again.

To be continued…

Natalie.

Chapter 5

The Letter

"Beryl!" Why does she have to shout that terrible name? "There's a letter here for somebody who calls herself Natalie!"

I had asked my mother to call me Natalie at least ten times and she said she would, but she never did. My dad, on the other hand, surprised me. "I never liked the name Beryl anyway," he said when I asked him to call me Natalie. "I had no say in naming you. Your mother called you Beryl after her rich great-aunt, and when the old tyrant died, she didn't leave you a penny. So a lot of good it did sticking you with that name."

The letter was from the T. Eaton Company telling me I had got the job at the candy counter and I was to report for work on Monday morning, July 17, at nine o'clock.

My mother wasn't too pleased about my job. "You be sure to tell them that you're only available until school starts in the fall," she said. "I want you to get your high-school diploma."

"I will," I promised.

But my first workweek was so hectic that I forgot to tell

anybody anything. There was so much to learn! How to fold bags and make boxes and how to use the weigh-scales and how to ring up the cash and make correct change. I couldn't get over how busy the candy counter was. It never ceased to amaze me how people would squander their sugar rations on Cottage Sweets—mostly to send to the boys overseas, of course.

Myra had got the typing job in the office. So we went back and forth to work together.

"How do you like your job, Myra?" I asked at the end of our first week. We were hanging onto the bar above our heads because the streetcar was so crowded we couldn't get a seat. Myra was trying to put on another coat of lipstick as the car joggled along the tracks.

"It's swell," she said, pressing her lips together. "And the pay's good, too."

"How much do you get?"

"Sixteen dollars a week."

"Sixteen! I only get fourteen."

"That's because office work is higher paying," she said proudly.

"At least us girls at the candy counter get to take home free broken chocolates," I shrugged.

On Saturday, July 22, I got my first pay envelope with my name, Natalie Brigham, typewritten on the flap of the small brown envelope. Inside were two five-dollar bills, a two, and two ones. When I got home, I handed my mother six dollars for board and she handed me back the one.

"Buy war savings stamps with it, Beryl," she said. "That way you'll be killing two birds with one stone—you'll be helping to 'lick' Hitler and you'll be saving for your future at the same time."

So, the very next Monday I told my supervisor, Miss Jackson, that I wanted to sign up for a dollar's worth of war savings stamps every week. The stamps cost twenty-five cents each and sixteen stamps (four dollars worth) filled a book.

Miss Jackson smiled her approval. "Good for you, Natalie!" she said. "And when your book is full I'll show you how to send it to Ottawa and you'll get a five dollar war savings sertificate back. Why, by the time the war is over, you'll be rich!"

"I wonder when that will be?" I thought as I got into my Cottage Sweets uniform (a frilly apron and cap like a maid in a movie). It seemed to me that it had been wartime forever. And to tell the truth I hadn't been very patriotic before Carmen went away. I used to complain all the time about blackouts. It seemed silly to have blackout curtains on our windows and no streetlights when the bombing was thousands of miles away. And I hated the food rationing because I liked lots of butter on my toast and sugar in my tea. But since Carmen left, those little things didn't seem to matter anymore.

Is this right ←

All the boys in our neighbourhood were disappearing one by one. Almost every other night we were seeing somebody off at Union Station.

"Whose turn is it this time, Natalie?" my dad asked as I primped at the kitchen mirror.

"I wish it was my turn," Rickey said. We called him Rickey because he was named after Dad, and Mom didn't like the sound of "little Richard" or "Junior." He was squinting down the barrel of his toy gun.

"Don't talk foolish," my mother said with a shudder.

"The Lambert triplets are leaving tonight," I told my dad. "They didn't want to be separated so they all joined the navy together."

"That'll be hard on their mother," remarked my mother. "Remember what happened to the Stewart twins last April? They both went down with their ship and their parents have never been the same since."

Myra and I went down to the station with Sylvia Lambert, the only girl in that family. Mr. and Mrs. Lambert were very brave as they kissed their sons goodbye at the station, but they cried all the way home on the streetcar. Sylvia sat alone and stared out the window into the black night.

Myra and I sat across the aisle from her. "I'm glad Rickey is only ten years old," I whispered. "I used to wish I had an older brother so he would bring his friends home. But not anymore."

"I'm glad I've only got sisters," Myra whispered back.

Chapter 6

Sunday, August 13, 1943

Dear Dolores:

I've decided to give you a name so it will be more like writing letters to a friend.

Aunt Marie came over after church waving a postcard from Carmen. It has a picture of a British bulldog on it wearing a Maple Leaf helmet and under it, in big red letters, it says, Carry On, Canada! Carmen's handwriting—he writes back slant—said, *Somewhere in England. In training for the big day.* (Then the next two lines were blacked out by the censor.) *Give my love to everybody back home. Carmen.*

That's all we've heard so far. Nothing for me yet and I've written him five long letters. I must admit (only to you, Dolores) that I am getting pretty jealous of all the letters Eloise receives from her "hubby."

Yours truly,
Natalie.

August 20, 1943

Dear Dolores:

Guess what? I am thinking of joining the CWAC (The Canadian Women's Army Corps). What gave me the idea was seeing Rachel Sinclair in uniform and she's only six weeks older than me. She lied about her age and joined up in hopes of going overseas where the boys are. I could do the same but I don't think my father would let me get away with it. I am still only seventeen by the calendar, and you can't call your soul your own until you're at least eighteen.

I might try to get a job at a munitions factory instead. Two girls I know work on the assembly line at Dominion Bridge. They make naval and artillery shells, and they get paid thirty-five dollars a week! That's more than twice as much as I make at the candy counter. And to tell the truth I'm getting sick of the smell of chocolate and I'm fed up with the frilly apron.

One day later:

Rachel came over all excited. Her corps is being transferred from Manning Pool in Toronto to the CWAC Depot in Kingston, Ontario. From there she expects to be shipped overseas.

We went up to my bedroom so I could try on her uniform. It didn't look as good on me as on Rachel because it didn't fit. Rachel is bigger than me…both ways. She told me all about what it's like in the army. She said the barracks are crowded and noisy, and some of the girls are as tough as men. Especially the officers. The more she talked the less the army appealed to me. Maybe I'd like the airforce better. I'll have to think about it.

>To be continued…
>Natalie.

Chapter 7

Dancing at the Armoury

"Where do you think you're off to, young lady?" My father was standing at the foot of the stairs watching me come down in my new two-piece red suit and black patent leather pumps.

"To a dance at the Armouries," I said. "I've already told Mother."

"Who are you going with?"

"Myra Adams."

"I haven't seen you with Eloise lately." Dad was partial to Eloise. He said she had a good head on her shoulders. "Have you two had a falling-out?"

"Course not. We're still best friends. It's just that now she's a married woman, she can't dance with other men. She says it wouldn't be fair to Jim. And he promised her he'd never even look at another girl while he's overseas."

"Good for him," Dad said. "Well, don't be late."

"I won't," I promised and ran out the door before he could tell me what he meant by late.

The Armoury was festooned with coloured balloons and red, white and blue paper streamers. Fine sawdust was spread all over the floor to make it slippery.

Myra and I were leaning against the wall by the door like a couple of wallflowers when Mart Kenny's band started playing "Serenade in Blue." Just then a tall sailor in a navy blue uniform and white middy blouse came striding across the floor towards us, his bell-bottomed trousers flaring out around his ankles.

"Wanna dance?" he asked me.

"Okay," I said and off we went, sliding through the saw-dust.

"What's your name, doll?" He had to lean down to reach my ear.

"Natalie Brigham," I said. "What's yours?"

"Ordinary Seaman Kenneth Roper," he said. "My friends call me Ken."

I tilted my head back and looked up into his handsome face. He sure didn't look ordinary to me.

I danced with lots of servicemen that night—soldiers and sailors and airforcemen. Then Ken cut in on the last dance and we ended the evening together.

At eleven o'clock the band struck up "There'll always be an England." You couldn't dance to it but we all joined hands and began swaying and singing lustily, "Red, white and blue...What does it mean to you? Show them you're proud...Shout it aloud...Britain's away..." Then the last piece they played was "God Save the King." Everybody stood stock-still and we sang it proudly with our arms straight down at our sides.

Ken walked Myra and me to the streetcar stop.

"Have you got a phone number?" he asked me.

"Melrose 6898," I answered promptly.

He repeated it, then promised to phone me before he got shipped out again. He was home on shore leave, he said.

I waved to him out the streetcar window. "Isn't he handsome?" I said. "And he must be at least twenty. Does he look twenty to you?"

Instead of answering, Myra said, "Will Ashby is going to be mad at you."

Myra didn't even like Will Ashby. She said I was crazy for going around with him. But I think she was a bit jealous because the soldier she had been dancing with hadn't even asked her for her phone number.

"I don't care," I said with a happy sigh. "I'm not the least bit interested in what Will Ashby thinks."

Chapter 8

Dear Dolores:

   He hasn't phoned yet. The sailor, I mean. And Will's
mad as hops just like Myra predicted. He is taking
another girl out—Ruby Slaughter. I couldn't care less,
honestly.

   I finally got a letter from Carmen. He sounds like
he's having a whale of a time over there. He is stationed
somewhere outside London, and when he has a weekend
pass he goes into London on the tube to the Service
Clubs and has a ball (his own words!). I thought
London would be all bombed-out buildings and air-raid
sirens, and everybody would be huddled in the
Underground. But Carmen says there are parties at the
Service Clubs every night of the week and our boys in
uniform are so popular with the English girls that they
make the British servicemen green with envy.

   I feel strangely rejected.
   Natalie.

Chapter 9

"School starts next week," my mother reminded me. "Have you given Eatons your notice yet?"

I had already made up my mind what I was going to do, but I hadn't told my parents yet. I was drying the dishes and I kept my eyes on the glass tumbler I was meticulously polishing when I blurted out, "I've decided to quit school."

Mom dropped the pot she was scrubbing into the dishpan with a splash. "You've what? You promised me, Beryl, that you'd finish high school."

"I know, but all my friends are going into war work. Myra and I met Joan Weston and Mary-Lou Eastwood on the streetcar coming home, and they told us they were making thirty-five dollars a week at Dominion Bridge. That's twice as much as we make at Eatons. And, besides, war work is patriotic."

"Well, I doubt if they'll take you on anyway because you're only seventeen," my mother said hopefully.

"You only have to be sixteen to quit school, Mother. You know that."

"What's this about quitting school?" My father looked up from his newspaper. He took one more puff of his daily cigarette and pinched it out and licked his finger. He only allowed himself one cigarette a day, two puffs at a time.

"Beryl says she's quitting school to do war work," my mother said as she dumped the contents of the dishpan with a swoosh down the sink.

"Wellll..." Dad surprised us both with his hesitation. "War workers are badly needed now that the able-bodied men are all gone or going. And I just heard that the John Inglis Company down on Strachan Avenue is hiring young women by the peck. They've stopped making washing machines and stoves altogether, and they're turning out machine guns by the thousands."

"Gee, thanks for the tip, Dad." I dropped the tea towel and ran into the dining room then grabbed the phone off the wall and twirled the dial.

"Myra," I said excitedly. "My dad says John Inglis is hiring young women by the peck."

"That's us!" she cried. "Let's go down there tomorrow."

Four of us from Eatons went down. Shannon Fraser, whose family had moved up recently from Nova Scotia, and Velma Morris and Myra and me. We all filled out applications and they hired us on the spot. But we still hadn't given in our notices at Eatons.

The next day we all went to our supervisors with the news. None of us got a reference because we had quit without giving notice. But we didn't really care because we were already hired at John Inglis.

The first thing we found out at John Inglis was that you had to have Registration Certificates to work there. (We hadn't needed them at Eatons because it wasn't war work so there was no need for "security".) The John Inglis Company gave us the first day off to get registered.

At the Registration Office in the City Hall a woman in a black uniform gave us each a card on which to print our vital statistics: name, address, birthdate and telephone number if applicable.

Some people didn't have telephones. But we did because my dad was a volunteer fireman. So many able-bodied young firemen had joined the armed forces that the fire department was mostly made up of middle-aged volunteers now.

"Are you going to lie about your name again?" hissed Myra.

"Sure," I hissed back. "It worked at Eatons. And Shannon and Velma think that's my real name already. It would only cause confusion if I changed it back."

"But this is a government document," Myra insisted. She was such a worrywart. "I think you can get in serious trouble if you lie on it."

"Well, it's too late now," I shrugged. I had already printed it with pen and ink, but I decided to add Beryl as my middle name.

Just then the woman in black gathered up our applications and quick-marched us down a long hall to a heavy, carved door. There was a plaque on the door which read

Office of the Registrar General. Behind a big wooden desk with a green blotter on it sat an important-looking man in uniform. He had a lined forehead and a grey moustache.

He turned out to be the Deputy Registrar of Canada. We had to sign our names in his presence, and then he signed his name under ours. As he handed our certificates back, duly witnessed, he gave us a solemn lecture. "Now then, young ladies," he said in a governmental voice, "You must never go anywhere without carrying your Registration Certificates on your persons. Is that understood?"

We nodded.

"Don't just nod your heads like puppets. Say, 'Yes sir', if you understand."

"Yes, sir," we said.

Then he continued, "Just remember, it is a serious offence for a war worker to be caught without this document."

"Yes, sir," we said in unison and I felt as if we should salute. He said, "You're dismissed." And the woman in black marched us down the hall and out the massive City Hall doors.

Chapter 10

Wonderful News

I wanted to look my best on the first day of my new job, so the night before, I pressed my spring suit (now my fall suit) and shampooed my hair.

My mother had managed to find an envelope of Lovalon Shampoo in Woolworth's, so my black hair felt wondrously soft as I did it up in pincurls in front of the kitchen mirror. I had just finished twisting the last curl when a knock came at the back door. It was Eloise and her dark eyes were all red and puffy from crying.

"What's the matter?" I cried, as I pulled her in the door. I looked down, my heart fluttering, half-expecting to see a telegram in her hands. "What's happened?"

She glanced around the kitchen furtively. "Are we alone?"

"Yes. My mother's at a Red Cross meeting and my father's working overtime. Rickey's in the basement playing with his machine gun." I pushed her into a chair and sat down opposite. "What is it, Eloise?"

"Oh," she sighed. "I have wonderful news."

"Wonderful news! Then why have you been crying?"

"Oh, Natalie. I think I'm going to have a baby!"

"A baby! Really? When?"

She began counting on her fingers: "June, July, August, September...sometime in February, I guess. Oh, Beryl...I mean Natalie...I'm thrilled and excited but...but..." Tears welled up in her eyes again. "I don't know if Jim will be happy about it because he said he didn't want to start a family until after the war."

"Oh, sure he'll be happy," I laughed. "Jim loves kids. Why he even likes my little brother."

"Who likes me?" asked Rickey, poking his head out the cellar door. His hair and face and hands were grey with coal dust.

"Nobody would like you the way you look right now," I laughed, tousling his ashy blond curls. "You smell like a coal man. Go upstairs and jump into the tub before Mom comes home."

We waited until he was out of earshot, then Eloise said, "I haven't even told my parents yet. You're the first to know."

"Why haven't you told them? Don't you think they'll be pleased?"

"I'm not sure. My mother was dead set against me marrying so young, you know."

"Yes, but she'll get over it. Quit worrying."

I put the kettle on the gas stove and lit it with a bang. Then I got a bag of apple blossom biscuits down from the shelf and put two on a plate and returned the bag to the shelf. My mother had given strict orders to eat them sparingly because they had cost her two sugar coupons.

Eloise was looking down at her stomach. Her plaid skirt was a bit tight around her middle. I hadn't noticed that before.

"I'm getting fat already," she said. "I won't be able to keep it a secret much longer."

"Well, then, tell your Mom and Dad tonight," I said. "It's good news, not bad."

"I wonder if it will be a boy or a girl?" Eloise patted her stomach affectionately. "I think I can feel it moving already."

"My mother says it's a girl if you feel life early," I said. "She says boys are lazy. She said she didn't feel a thing from Rickey until the seventh month. By the way, have you thought of any names?"

Eloise smiled dreamily. "Well, if it's a boy I guess we'll have to call him James. James Foster the Third. Jim's dad's name is James too you know."

"Well, then, let's hope it's a girl. How about calling her Natalie after your best friend?"

Just then Mother and Dad came in the door together. "Where's your brother?" asked my mother.

"He's in the bathtub," I said. We heard sloshing from above.

"Hello there, Eloise. How are you?" Dad gave Eloise a big smile.

"I'm fine, Mr. Brigham." She was smiling now, too. "But I'd better be going. I have something important to tell my parents. Goodnight!"

My mother raised her eyebrows as the door shut. "What's that all about?" she asked.

"Umm. What's what all about? I don't know what you mean."

Then I saw a glint in her eye. "I think you just told me," she grinned.

"Told you what?" Dad asked.

"Curiosity killed the cat," Mom teased.

"Oh, bosh!" Dad said and he went into the living room to listen to the war news on our mantle radio.

Chapter 11

Nov. 11, 1943
Remembrance Day

Dear Dolores:

Today the whole city of Toronto was silent for two minutes in honour of our war dead of the Great War (the war
to end all wars). At exactly eleven o'clock, all traffic and
streetcars stopped in their tracks, and in factories like
John Inglis, all machinery came to a dead halt. You could
have heard a hairpin drop. This year special prayers were
said, not only for the dead of the Great War, but for the
many boys who have already been sacrificed in the war
still raging in Europe. Sacrificed! What a terrible word.

Natalie.

Nov. 15, 1943

Dear Dolores:

I meant to write to you more often. But now that I'm a
war worker I'm either too tired or too busy. I've been at
John Inglis for almost two months now and at last I feel
like I'm an important part of the war effort. A cog in the

wheel you might say. A little cog in a big wheel. But, as my dad says, "Every cog has got its work cut out."

I have already filled two war savings books with stamps and I've applied for a Victory Bond. That's one way to help win the war I guess. But it doesn't compare to actually making ammunition like bullets and bombs. That's real war work and I find it positively exhilarating.

Natalie.

November 19, 1943

Dear Dolores:

Boy was I tired when I got home tonight. I was on the assembly line all day making shell casings. It's hard work and dirty, too. My fingernails are black with grease every night and I have to scrape them clean with Dad's penknife before I take a bath.

The plant is a very noisy, exciting and interesting place to work. We start at 8:00 a.m. sharp. And we dress entirely different than in civilian life. We change each morning in the ladies' room from our street clothes to our work clothes. We wear coveralls and short-sleeved blouses and bandanas tied in a topknot around our hair. It's a nice change from the frilly maid's uniform I had to wear at the candy counter. We work alongside lots of men—the men are either too old or have flat feet, or some other defect that prevents them from joining the armed forces. Most of the men are fun and flirty, but some of them really resent working with girls and women and are very sarcastic. One man in particular, Buck Bronson, who is forty years old if he's a day, said that he'd knock his wife's block off if he ever caught her wearing the pants in the family. Well, that made me see red. So I told him that if I were his wife I'd knock his block off first. Well, lucky for me our supervisor, Bill Sergeant, who is a World War One vet and an air-raid warden at night, overheard Bronson's remark and gave him a good dressing down. He said that to wear skirts and loose hair around dangerous machinery would jeopardize our safety. So we girls won that round. But I'll have to learn to keep my mouth shut because I don't want to make enemies or get fired. I have to go to bed now. I'm dead beat.

Natalie.

Chapter 12

Ditty Bags

"Marie's coming over tonight and we're going to pack ditty bags for the boys overseas," Mom said. "We want to get them off early so they'll be in time for Christmas. Would you like to help, Beryl?"

"Sure," I said. "How about I ask Eloise? She hasn't heard from Jim in two weeks and she's getting frantic."

"That's a good idea. It'll make her feel better, doing something special for her hubby. And it should cheer Marie up too."

Aunt Marie has been down in the dumps lately. "She's missing Carmen something terrible these days. He doesn't write her nearly often enough," my mother said. "That's what comes of having an only child. You're too wrapped up in them. I wish she'd get a job or do some volunteer work for the Red Cross. She needs something to take her mind off herself."

We put two leaves in the dining-room table so there would be lots of room for us to work. Then we made four ditty bags—one for Carmen, of course, and one for my mother's brother Terrence, who was in the ground crew of the RCAF, serving in Bagotville, Quebec. And another cousin, Walter Gilmore, who is in the Navy, and one for Private James Foster, Eloise's hubby and father-to-be. (Eloise said she had told Jim about the baby in her last letter but she hadn't heard back from him yet.)

In each ditty bag we put a pound box of Cottage Sweets, a tin of fruitcake, biscuits shaped like Christmas bells, licorice allsorts, razor blades, two flat fifties of Wings Cigarettes (Wings are the favourite of the armed forces) and knitted socks, mitts and mufflers that my mother and Aunt Marie had made. When the canvas bags were stuffed full, we pulled the drawstrings tight, then packed them into corrugated cartons and covered them with Christmas stickers.

My mother moistened her lips, which were dry from licking stickers. "Now, let's have tea in the kitchen," she said. "I think we've earned it."

We sat around the kitchen table, sipping tea and eating broken biscuits that we hadn't deemed good enough for the ditty bags.

"Would anybody like to see the last postcard I got from my hubby?" Eloise reached into her left-hand blouse pocket, where she carried the card next to her heart, and handed it to me.

On it was a picture of a baby in a diaper and steel helmet, dropping out of the sky in a parachute with a Tommy gun cradled in his arms. Under the picture was the caption Help him win the war. Buy Victory Bonds.

I turned it over and started to read Jim's message out loud. "Dear, sweet darling…"

"For pity's sake, Beryl," Eloise was blushing like a school-girl, "read it to yourself."

I have to admit that I felt a wave of jealousy over the endearing words. I had never been called "darling" by anybody in my entire life, never mind "sweet darling." There was no mention of the baby so Eloise's letter and Jim's postcard must have crossed paths as they made their way across the ocean.

Then Aunt Marie pulled Carmen's last letter out of her handbag and spread it on the table so we could all see it at once. We could barely believe our eyes. It was so heavily censored that we could hardly make head or tail of what he was trying to tell us. But we did manage to make out, with the help of a magnifying glass, the very last words: *Mission Accomplished*.

"What could that mean?" Aunt Marie said in a small voice.

There was no answer to her question.

Chapter 13

December 16, 1943, Will's Birthday

Dear Dolores:

Will Ashby celebrated his eighteenth birthday on Saturday. I was invited to his house for a birthday supper and then we went to the show (another war picture!). The following Monday, true to his word, he went down to the recruiting station and joined up. His mother had a fit and his father was furious. Mr. Ashby had lost a leg below the knee in the Great War and now he was afraid of losing his only son.

I must say the army uniform has done wonders for Will. He looks almost handsome. And he says the army is going to fix his teeth before he goes overseas. So that should be an improvement. Also, he asked me if I'd be his girl again. And will I wait for him. "What about Ruby Slaughter?" I asked. "Oh, her," he said. "I just dated her to make you jealous." So I said I'd be his girl again but I hesitated about the waiting. "After all, I am only seventeen," I said, and for once I was glad of the excuse. But just the same it is nice having a boyfriend again. Especially one in uniform.

Sincerely,
Natalie.

Chapter 14

Christmas Company

Mother and Rickey and I were sitting at the supper table eating meatless stew —we had used up our week's meat ration in three days—when I noticed a secretive smile flitting across Mom's face.

"What's that all about?" I asked, using her words.

"What's what all about?" she smirked.

"That grin. What have you got up your sleeve?"

"Her arm!" Rickey said. Ever since he turned ten, he's become a real smart aleck.

"Guess what I did today," Mother said, still smirking.

"Tell us," I said. "I'm too tired for guessing games." It had been a hard day down at the plant and I had worked an hour of overtime, which was swell because overtime paid double.

Mother put her fork down. "Guess who's coming to our house for Christmas dinner?" she said all in one breath.

"Who?" I demanded impatiently.

"Yeah, who?" echoed Rickey.

"Well, last week Mrs. Penrose and I went down to

Manning Pool and put our names in to invite two overseas servicemen for Christmas dinner. And today I got a phone call saying that a British soldier and an RAF Flying Officer had accepted my invitation."

"Really? Wow! That's wonderful. Can I ask Myra to come?"

"Well, yes, but what about her family dinner?"

"Oh, they always have it at noon hour."

"Then tell her she's welcome. That'll make eight for dinner, including Marie." Aunt Marie and Carmen had always had Christmas dinner with us since Uncle Farley disappeared. "It will be our first Christmas without Carmen," my mother said wistfully. "I hope having servicemen with us will help cheer Marie up."

It might do the opposite, I thought. But I didn't say so. We had received a nice Christmas card from Carmen. It had a picture of Santa Claus wearing a Canadian Army helmet set against the Union Jack. Under the picture were the words, Merry Christmas Canada! Then on the other side Carmen had written that he had received our ditty bag and had shared it with all his crew. He also said not to worry about him. With luck, he would soon be home.

Instead of cheering me up his brave words sent cold shivers down my spine.

Myra came over about four o'clock in the afternoon Christmas day. She was wearing a green velvet suit, which did wonders for her green eyes and auburn hair. I was wearing a blue wool dress, which I hoped did the same for my blue eyes and black hair.

Myra helped me set the table with our good china and silver plate. In the middle of the sparkling white tablecloth we had made a wreath out of twigs and pine cones from the evergreen on our front lawn. We put a red candle in silver holders (Aunt Marie's wedding gift to my mother) at each end of the table. The candlesticks were only used on special occasions. And this sure was a special occasion!

We took one last look at ourselves in the hall mirror, and then we sat on the chesterfield in the living room with our ankles crossed, waiting breathlessly.

"I asked my parents to call me Natalie today," I said. "And they said they would. Boy, I sure hope they remember."

"Well, I promise I'll remember," said Myra. "But what about Rickey?"

"Oh, I bribed him with twenty-five cents. He'll do anything for money."

Just then a knock came at the front door. "Will you get that, Beryl?" my mother yelled from the kitchen.

"Mother!"

"I mean Natalie. Will you answer the door, Natalie?"

I ran to the door with Myra at my heels and opened it to two of the most gorgeous boys…men…I'd ever seen in my life.

Christmas, 1943, promised to be memorable. Both our servicemen were handsome. But only one was extraordinarily handsome. His name was Flying Officer Reginald Anderson and he had a gorgeous English accent that reminded me of Ronald Colman, the movie star.

We took to each other at first sight. You could even say sparks flew. So Myra had to settle for the British soldier whose name was Corporal Andrew Martin. He was nice looking, too, but not extraordinary.

My mother managed to produce a marvellous turkey dinner with all the trimmings because we had studiously saved our meat and sugar and butter rations for the big day.

"May I be so bold as to ask for seconds, Mrs. Brigham?" asked Reggie. He had told me that's what his friends called him—Reggie.

"Why, of course," my mother said, passing the bowls. "But be sure to save room for plum pudding." Then she added diffidently, "It probably won't be as good as you're used to back home. I understand the English are experts at plum pudding."

Well, at the end of the meal both Reggie and Andrew said it was the most delicious Christmas dinner they'd ever eaten in their lives. Particularly the plum pudding.

After the washing-up Myra and I settled the blackout curtains on the windowsills. Then we all gathered around the tree, which was sparkling with gold and silver garlands but no electric lights. Electric lights were forbidden for the duration.

I turned the radio on and as the tubes warmed up, the

lovely strains of "Silent Night, Holy Night" filled the air. After more familiar carols, the announcer said, "The next two songs are dedicated to our English comrades training here in Canada."

Then the beautiful voice of Vera Lynn filled the room. "There'll be bluebirds over, the white cliffs of Dover..." and "When the lights go on again, all over the world..." There wasn't a dry eye in our living room.

After a final cup of tea and dark fruitcake, our servicemen thanked my parents profusely for the unforgettable Christmas (their words). Then Corporal Andrew Martin gallantly escorted Myra across the street and I was left standing with Flying Officer Reginald Anderson in the hallway. Dangling from the hall-light fixture (the light was turned off to conserve electricity) hung a sprig of mistletoe.

Glancing up, Reggie grinned. "May I kiss you goodnight, Natalie?" he said in a romantic whisper.

I looked up into his blue English eyes (shyly I hoped) and whispered back, "Yes, Reggie."

He kissed me like I have never been kissed before.

"I hope we meet again, Natalie," he said.

"I hope so, too," I said.

Chapter 15

Caught Red-handed

"Mother!" I called from the door as I stamped the snow off my galoshes on the hall mat. "You'll never believe what happened to me on the way home from work tonight."

"What?" She came running down the hall, wiping her hands on her apron. "Are you all right, Beryl?"

I couldn't expect her to remember my change-of-name under the circumstances. "I am now," I said, hanging up my snowy coat and hat on the wall rack. "But I came this close," I held my thumb and finger about one inch apart, "to getting arrested."

"Arrested! What on earth for? What did you do?"

"I got caught red-handed by a Home Guard without my Registration Certificate. I must have left it on the dresser this morning when I changed purses. And if Myra hadn't been with me to verify who I was, I don't know where I'd be right now. Probably behind bars. But Myra swore I was Natalie Brigham and where I worked, and she showed the guard *her* Registration Card. So he said he'd let me off with a warning this time. But he made me swear that I'd never, ever go anywhere without my Registration Certificate again. 'You could be a spy or a subversive for all I know,' he said."

"Well, for heaven's sakes," my mother said, shaking her head as she went back to the kitchen. "You'd think he'd have more to do." Then she pointed to the hall table. "There's a postcard for you."

I grabbed it up and looked at the picture first. I was expecting to see an English scene, like Piccadilly Circus or King George reviewing his troops, but instead it was a picture of a troop ship in Halifax harbour.

Dear Natalie, said the bold handwriting. *Didn't have time to phone. Sorry. Being shipped back to England tomorrow morning on the HMCS* Cordova. *I will keep your phone number next to my heart in case I ever get back to Canada. With fondest memories, Reggie.*

I sighed so loudly my mother said, "What's the matter?"

"Oh, I'm just sick of being left behind all the time," I said.

"I know how you feel," she said. "It was the same for my generation. I guess we'll never learn."

I read the card again. I was surprised at how heartbroken his words made me feel. After all, I had only known Reggie for one day. But I will never forget that memorable kiss under the mistletoe as long as I live.

I turned the card over and looked at the picture again to see if the ship was indeed the HMCS *Cordova* but it wasn't.

It was the HMCS *Moosejaw*. In the corner of the card were two flags crossed—the Union Jack and the Canadian Ensign. I couldn't help wondering (and hoping) that it was a secret message from Reggie.

Chapter 16

De Havilland

I was coming home on the streetcar by myself because Myra had gone someplace with her new friend, Marion Baker. I had hung around with them for a couple of weeks but I soon felt like a third wheel. Halfway home I got a seat by the window so I opened my new book, *Random Harvest*, by James Hilton and I was soon lost in it. A few minutes later a man sat down beside me. I could tell by a glimpse of his trousers that he was a civilian so I didn't bother to look up. Then a masculine voice interrupted my reading.

"Good book, Beryl?" he asked.

He knew my name—my awful name—so I glanced sideways to see who it was. It was Carl Monroe, a boy I used to know in high school.

"Oh, hi, Carl," I said. Instantly I wondered why he wasn't in uniform. Anybody *not* in uniform was automatically suspect. He read my mind.

"I'm deaf in one ear," he said, tapping the left side of his head. "I tried to get in all the forces, but I couldn't pass the hearing test."

I could tell he was embarrassed so I changed the subject.

"Are you working?" I asked.

"Yep. At De Havilland."

"I'm at John Inglis," I said proudly.

"De Havilland pays better," he said.

My ears perked up. "How much to start? For a girl—I mean a woman?"

"Well, my sister's making forty dollars a week and she's only been there two months. I'm a foreman now so I could probably hire you on."

"What kind of work would I be doing?"

"Right now we're turning out Mosquitoes. No other bomber compares to it—it's so light and fast. We can't build them quick enough."

"Sounds exciting," I said. "But, isn't De Havilland out of town? Way up in Downsview? How would I get there?"

"Car pool," he said. "I've got room for one more in my Dodge two-door. It's nearly a two mile walk to Wilson Avenue from the plant."

"How come you're on the streetcar today?" I said.

He laughed. "No flies on you," he quipped. "Had a flat tire this morning but I'll have it fixed by tonight."

He glanced out the streetcar window. "Here's my stop," he said. "Why don't you give me your phone number?" I scrabbled in my purse for a pencil and jotted my phone number down on an old transfer. I handed it to Carl just as he got up to leave at Shaw Street. "I'll call you," he said as he jumped out the streetcar door.

I could hardly wait to get home and talk it over with my parents. Now that Myra Adams and her new friend were so chummy I often had to ride home alone. And I was sick and tired of the assembly line at John Inglis. The men there were all old and ugly.

I waited to broach the subject until my dad came in.

"I met Carl Monroe on the streetcar," I said. "He sat beside me."

"Is he home on leave?" Dad asked, passing the hot casserole. Mom had made macaroni and cheese for supper because the meat rations were all gone for another week.

"No. He's not in the armed forces because he's deaf in one ear," I explained. "He works at De Havilland Aircraft and he says he can get me a job there. I could probably make thirty-five dollars a week."

"Oh, my," my mother said, scraping the crispy brown edge of the casserole onto Rickey's plate. "That's a lot of money for a girl."

"Well, a bird in the hand is worth two in the bush," Dad said. "So don't go quitting one job until you're sure you've got the other one." Dad had been out of work for nearly a year during the Great Depression, so steady work meant a lot to him.

The very next night the phone rang. Dad answered it and called from the dining room, "It's for you, Beryl!"

It was Carl Monroe. "Hi there, Beryl," he said. "I've got you a job interview Saturday morning. How does that sound?"

"Great," I said. "Where will I meet you?"

"I'll pick you up at the corner of College and Gladstone at 7:00 a.m. sharp. Okay?"

"Okay," I said. "Thanks, Carl. Bye."

"I think I've got the job at De Havilland," I told my parents.

"They're making those new fighter planes there," Dad said. "The Mosquito." I could tell he was impressed.

"The little twin-engine bomber is De Havilland's pride and joy," said Dad. "They say it turned the tide for Britain, just when it looked like Hitler would win the war and we would all have to learn to speak German. It's so small and fast that sometimes it isn't even equipped with defensive armament, cannons or rockets—just loaded up with as many bombs as the B17, which is a bigger, slower plane. It carries only two men, which is a darn sight better than nine, if it goes down. Our airmen flew raids in and out of enemy territory before the Luftwaffe could catch the little 'Mossies' bombing Gestapo headquarters. Once they even rescued one hundred Frenchmen at Amiens who were about to be executed the very next day. They bombed the prison walls with dead accuracy, freeing the POWs inside like Joshua did in the Bible, so it was called Operation Jericho. It wasn't all fun and games though. They flew so low to the ground that one poor fella crashed into a flag pole!"

All this, Dad told me, beaming with pride. I was flabbergasted by the stories and amazed that my dad knew so much more than I did, which left me a little deflated, I have to admit, considering that I was a soon-to-be employee of De Havilland Aircraft.

Carl's 1937 Dodge two-door was right there at 7:00 a.m. sharp. It was packed to the gills with young men and women. They shoved over and made room for me in the back seat. All told there were six of us.

"This is Beryl Brigham," Carl waved his hand at me over his shoulder. I nodded and smiled as I hunched up and squashed in.

Carl parked in front of a big sign, which read in huge letters, De Havilland Aircraft of Canada. Through the wide-open hangar doors I could see greenish-brown wings.

"First I'll take you upstairs to the office to fill out your application." he said to me. "Then I'll show you around the plant."

I blew some pink eraser bits off of the completed form and handed it to Carl.

"Natalie. That's a nice name," he said. "I always thought your name was Beryl."

"I'd rather be called Natalie," I said firmly.

"Fine by me," he said and introduced me to everybody. Then he turned me over to a big smiling woman in a polka dot bandana. "Natalie...this is Morag Turner. She'll show you the ropes."

Morag took me all over the plant and let me observe the women at work. We paused to watch some girls "doping" a

Mosquito fuselage. They stretched and glued fabric over the plywood frame like skin over a gaunt skeleton, with the outline of the seams showing through like ribs. Then we went into a large room where women were working on the huge wing, which was made all in one piece. They were gluing the fabric onto the frame, three wooden box spars with built-up ribs and stringers and a covering of laminated plywood strips running diagonally. The girls looked like an army of nurses in uniforms and masks, working on a giant patient suspended, huge and helpless, on supports. They were brushing on dope, a clear lacquer, to seal the cloth. Afterwards, Morag explained, it would be painted camouflage green/brown in another part of the plant before it rolled out into the daylight, ready to take to the skies. But it was light and hollow, nonetheless, and I couldn't help but blurt out how flimsy it looked—this would carry our boys thousands of feet into the air! Morag just shrugged and told me that they weren't built to last. The lifespan of a Mosquito was often only days. My stomach went queasy when it dawned on me what she meant. I had to stop myself from imagining the plane spiralling downward with smoke pouring from the tail and our boys trapped inside.

On the following Monday I quit my job at John Inglis even though the boss offered me a raise.

"Why did you quit?" asked Myra at lunchtime. "I hope you're not mad at me for making friends with Marion Baker."

I laughed. "No, I'm not mad, Myra. I'd just rather make airplanes than shells and bullets."

We had lunch together then, meatless sandwiches, and we parted still good friends.

I started work at De Havilland the next day and I loved every minute of it. Morag was a great teacher and I was a quick learner. Morag said so herself. By the end of the first day I knew I was born to be a doper. I was actually making Mosquitoes! The fastest airplane in the world with a cruising speed of 210 miles per hour! I knew that very first day that I would be working at De Havilland for the rest of the war...however long that might be.

Chapter 17

The Dambusters

At last a letter came from Carmen. It was postmarked London, England, but I couldn't tell whom it was from before I opened it because the envelope was written in girlish handwriting. I guess that's why it slipped past the censors. There wasn't a word blacked out.

Feb. 16, 1944

Dear Beryl,

How is everybody back there in Canada? I hope my mother is getting along okay without me. I know Aunt Jean and Uncle Jack (my parents) *will look out for her.*

I have exciting news, Beryl. I have been selected to join a special duties squadron in the RAF called "The Dambusters." I begin training tomorrow. I can hardly believe my luck. I'll be the youngest nose-gunner in a Lancaster Bomber. Don't tell my mother that because she might worry. But I know I'll be okay because my commander, Flying Officer Bob Brand, says I'm the best darn gunner in the airforce so for sure I'll get Jerry before he gets me.

I can just hear you asking, "What's a dambuster?" Well, I'll try to explain. *Dambusters are exactly that; it is our special duty to bust three specific dams in the Ruhr Valley in Germany.*

I'll have more to tell you after I've flown a few missions. I'm taking a chance that this news will get through uncensored because a pretty English girl, whose name is Joan, has offered to address the envelope for me so it will look like a civilian letter. If you get it uncensored, let me know. Say something like "I received your smashing good news" and I'll know what you mean. Then I'll tell you more about what's going on over here. I'll get my girlfriend to address all my letters from now on. I must sign off now, Beryl. Reveille is at 6:00 a.m. and I want to be sharp as a tack for my first day of training.

P.S. Don't show this letter to my mother.

> *Love to all,*
> *Carmen.*

I was rereading the letter after supper and curiously examining the girlish handwriting on the envelope. Carmen had called Joan his girlfriend. And even though Carmen was my cousin once removed and not my boyfriend, I felt a wave of jealousy wash over me. Well, at least, I thought, he hasn't got a Canadian girlfriend so Joan is not breaking anybody's heart back here at home. So many of my friends had lost boyfriends overseas—if not to the war then to some English girl waiting for them like vultures.

As I slipped the letter back into its envelope, my mother looked up from her knitting. She was always knitting something in khaki or airforce blue. "Who's your letter from, Beryl?"

"It's from Carmen," I said.

"It didn't look like his handwriting," Mother said. "I thought it was probably from your friend, Rachel, because the writing is so feminine."

"It's from Carmen, but he got his girlfriend to address the envelope in hopes of fooling the censors. And it worked. There's not a word blacked out."

"His girlfriend?" Mother dropped a stitch. "We'd better not tell your Aunt Marie that." She held the half-knitted sock closer to the twenty-five watt light bulb in the table lamp and began searching for the stitch. "I wish I could use a bigger bulb," she said. "This saving electricity is going to be the ruination of my eyes." She found the stitch, finished the row, rolled up the half-sock and put it in her knitting bag. "Well, what does Carmen have to say?" she asked.

Carmen had not said, Don't show your parents. Still, I handed the letter to my mother reluctantly. After she read it she clucked her tongue and passed it on to my father. He read it and gave it back to me.

"She should be told," my father said. I knew he meant Aunt Marie. "Just in case."

"In case of what?" The words caught in my mother's throat.

"In case the worst happens," my father said. "It's a dangerous mission he's going on."

"He'll come back," I insisted. "And you *can't* tell Aunt Marie. I promised and he trusts me."

At that very moment Aunt Marie came bursting in the kitchen door, waving her own letter. Dad took her coat and hat, shook off the snow and hung it on the cellar door. Aunt Marie blew snowflakes off the letter and handed it to me. It was full of love and laughter. Not a word about the Dambusters.

Mother made tea. Aunt Marie had brought a half-cup of sugar covered with waxed paper to keep it dry. She always brought her own sugar because she knew our sugar rations were in short supply. That's because my mother baked more than Aunt Marie.

"I'll excuse myself and go down to the cellar to work on my bicycle," Dad said. "Are you coming, little Richard?"

"Sure." To Dad's delight Rickey had inherited his mechanical ability. Rickey had even fixed the kitchen clock once— there were six pieces left over and it still worked like a charm.

Dad was getting his bicycle ready for spring. Our car, a 1929 Buick, was stored in the garage for the winter. Maybe for the duration, Dad had said. What with gasoline and oil rationing and balding tires, he had decided to bike it to work as soon as the good weather came. Meantime he rides the Red Rocket. That's the streetcar's nickname; but it was poorly named, Dad said, because it was slow as molasses in January. He was sure, come spring, he would make better time on his bicycle.

"I think I'll go upstairs and get ready for bed," I said. "I'm tired from doping all day." They laughed as I kissed them goodnight.

I had a small bath (the water was barely warm) because

the fire in the furnace had to be kept low to save on coal and we depended on the coil above the fire pit in the furnace to heat our water. Like everything else, coal was rationed because it was needed for the munitions factories.

I dried off, shivering—goosebumps from head to toe—and got into my flannelette nightgown and kimono. Next I did my hair up in pincurls with black bobby pins, then I got out my writing pad.

Dear Carmen I wrote. *I got your "smashing news." I did not show it to your mother but I had to show it to my parents, but don't worry I swore them to secrecy.*

Did I tell you in my last letter that I've changed jobs? I met an old high-school friend, Carl Monroe (you don't know him, he's a civvy because he's deaf in one ear), and he got me on at De Havilland Aircraft. I am making thirty-five dollars a week. Can you believe it? I am a doper and I am helping build Mosquitoes. If I can I'll have your name put on one. Have you ever flown one?

It is hard to think of something to say because nothing exciting happens here in Canada. Mother says we should be thankful for that, but it's boring. She also told me to tell you that she is doing her bit for the war effort by saving grease (pots and pots of it!) to help fry Hitler and we are strictly sticking to our rations so you boys over there can have lots of good food. We are required to eat three slices of bread at each meal to save our rations. That means lots of meatless stew and sugarless pie. (What could be more boring?) But I know I shouldn't complain, Carmen, especially to you. We are also buying war savings stamps and Victory

Bonds. *And your mother is investing all the money you send her in Victory Bonds so you'll be rich when you get home.*

Hey, who is this Joan-girl who mailed your letter? You called her your girlfriend. Are you serious? I think your mother wants you to come home by yourself, Carmen. Well, tell me more in your next "missile." Take care of yourself.

Love,
Natalie.

Dear Dolores:

I am very worried about Carmen. My father is too, and that's a bad sign. He is not a worrier. Mother and Aunt Marie are the worriers. I guess I take after them. I'll say a long prayer tonight.

I had to work overtime today to fill my quota. It was dark and cold and took forever go get home. I had to take the streetcars because Carl had run out of gas and won't get his new gas-ration book until Monday. I met Syd Snider walking down the street. He's home on embarkation leave. He's a sergeant in the army and he's leaving Friday night. He asked me to come down to Union Station to see him off. I said I would, but I am getting tired of always being left behind. The boys go off all waving and happy, and we girls go home all sad and lonely. I'm sick of it.

Bye, Dolores.
Natalie.

Chapter 18

Eloise's Baby

I was sitting buffing my nails at the kitchen table. Much as I liked my work on Mosquitoes it sure was hard on the fingernails. And you couldn't buy nail polish for love nor money, so it was hard to keep your hands looking nice. Just then the kitchen door burst open and Eloise Wilkinson, I mean Foster—I keep forgetting—blew in on a gust of cold March wind.

"BERYL!" she cried. I was just about to correct her when I saw the panic in her eyes.

"What's the matter?" I asked, jumping up.

"Where's your mother?"

"She's at the movies with my father. Why? What's the matter?"

Then she whispered, "Where's your brother?"

"He's upstairs in bed. It's ten o'clock. Why?"

"I think my baby's coming."

"You do? How can you tell? Where are your parents?"

"They're at my aunt's. It's their euchre night."

"Here." I dumped Rickey's collection of comic books off the chair beside the stove. "Come sit by the fire. You're shivering."

I took off her coat, which she had thrown carelessly over her shoulders, and pressed her into the chair beside the Quebec heater.

Dad had resurrected the Quebec heater from the garage and set it up in the kitchen so we would use less coal in the furnace. Coal was scarce these days because it was needed in factories like The Steel Company of Canada. Dad said the munitions factories practically ate it up by the ton.

"Oh, Beryl! I mean Natalie. I need help!" Eloise was clutching her big stomach and I could see she was in pain.

"What's your aunt's telephone number?" I asked her.

"She doesn't have one. Oh, Beryl, what'll I do?" Tears were pooling in her huge brown eyes and spilling down her cheeks.

"What hospital are you booked in?"

"Women's College," she gasped. "But how will I get there?"

I thought frantically, If only I knew how to drive, but the Buick was up on blocks with the wheels off anyway.

"C'mon," I said. "Let's get dressed. We're going to the hospital." I made a mad dash for the hall closet. I had extra hats and boots and scarves in there.

In five minutes I had us both bundled up and out the front door.

We lived just steps from the College carstop, and the sidewalk had been sanded so it wasn't too slippery. But I hung onto Eloise for dear life all the same.

Luckily a streetcar came along just in time. The streetcar driver was a woman in a TTC uniform. A lot of drivers were women now because the men had been drafted into the armed forces. I got behind Eloise and boosted her up the steps.

The driver took in the situation at a glance. "Women's College?" she asked. Women's College Hospital was on the College car line.

"Yes," I gasped. Eloise was heavy as a horse. "Can you hurry?"

"Leave the driving to me, kiddo." She gave us an encouraging smile. "You just get her into a seat. I don't want her falling on my shift."

She waited patiently until Eloise and I were safely seated. Then she took off like a rocket. I've never seen a streetcar move so fast. She whizzed right by the crowded streetcar stops, bells clanging, and left the people staring after us, dumbfounded.

She didn't stop until we were as close as she could get to the hospital. Then she got out and helped me walk Eloise, moaning all the way, across the road to the hospital door.

"Good luck," she said. "And God bless."

"Thank you!" I called back to her. Then I steered Eloise through the revolving doors.

The minute we got inside I felt safe. The hospital lobby was serenely quiet. Eloise breathed an audible sigh of relief.

"Are you all right?" I asked her.

"I think so," she answered breathlessly.

A nurse came over with a wheelchair and we lowered Eloise into it.

"You go to Admitting and give them the details," she ordered me, pointing to another nurse behind a counter, "and I'll take care of our patient." She looked down at Eloise, who suddenly seemed like a little girl instead of a soon-to-be mother.

"Where are you taking her?" I called after them as they whizzed across the floor to the elevator.

"Third Floor! Obstetrics!" she called back. Then the elevator doors closed on a wild-eyed Eloise.

I went to the counter and leaned on it with both arms. The nurse smiled and waited for me to catch my breath. Then she asked the questions—patient's name, age, address, husband's name.

"Private James Foster," I said.

"Where is he? He should be here!" she said.

"He's overseas," I said.

"Oh." She nodded knowingly. "Are you her sister?"

"No. I'm her best friend." I felt guilty saying that because I hadn't seen much of Eloise lately. I had been so busy with work and new friends at De Havilland.

"Where are her parents, then?"

"At her aunt's playing cards. But they have no phone."

"What kind of parents would leave a girl at a time like this?"

"Oh, they're wonderful parents. But the baby's two weeks early," I said.

"Well, has she got a brother?"

"No." The word "brother" reminded me of Rickey. "Oh my gosh," I said. "I've left my little brother home alone. Can I use your telephone?"

She handed me the receiver of the upright phone and I dialed our number. After about ten rings Rickey answered sleepily. "Are you alone?" I asked.

"I guess." I heard him yawn. "Where are you?"

"I'm at the hospital with Eloise," I explained. I looked at my Bulova wristwatch, which I had got on my last birthday. It was eleven o'clock. "Mother and Dad will be home soon. Tell them—"

"Here they come now," Rickey said. "Mom it's Beryl. She's at some hospital—"

"BERYL!" My mother had grabbed the phone before Rickey could explain. "What's happened?"

"Nothing bad, Mother. Eloise's baby started to come and I helped her to the hospital."

"For mercy sakes, how did you get her there?"

"By streetcar."

"Streetcar! Oh, Beryl. Is she all right?"

"I guess so. The nurse took her up to Obstetrics. Will you

tell the Wilkinsons? They should be home by now."

"I'll go right over. But how will you get home?"

"Tell her to take a cab," I heard my father say.

"I haven't got enough money with me. Tell Dad I'll take the streetcar."

"She says she hasn't enough money. She'll take the streetcar."

"Give me the phone." My dad came on the line. "You take a cab. I'll pay for it," he said, and hung up.

"How do I get a taxicab?" I asked the nurse at the desk.

"I'll call one for you," she said and picked up the phone.

"But I'd like to see Eloise before I leave," I said.

"Not allowed." She shook her head decisively. "Husbands and mothers only."

I got in the cab and gave my address. It was my first cab ride and I was thrilled. I told the cabbie all about what had happened.

"Well, I hope your friend has a boy for her soldier husband," he said.

"Well, I hope it's a girl," I said indignantly, "for herself."

My father was at the curb in front of our house. He paid the fare and just as my taxi pulled away, Mr. and Mrs. Wilkinson drove up and parked in front of their house, which was attached to ours.

"What's going on?" Mr. Wilkinson looked surprised to see us standing on the curb in the cold.

"I took Eloise to the hospital," I said. "The baby's coming."

"OH! OH! OH!" cried Mrs. Wilkinson.

"Get back in the car, Mother," her husband said. And they drove off at top speed.

James Foster the Third came into the world at six o'clock the next morning. My mother and I went down at evening visiting hours. They didn't want to let us in because we're not blood-related to the new mother, but the nurse at Admitting remembered me and she made an exception.

Mrs. Wilkinson was there, chittering like a mother hen.

Eloise was sitting up in bed, glowing. "I would have named him Natalie if he'd been a girl," she said. "But Jim will be pleased he's got a namesake."

My mother kissed Eloise on the cheek and then arranged the flowers we had brought in a vase.

Eloise looked so wonderful compared to the wretched girl I had brought to the hospital the night before that I just had to ask her the big question, "Was it very bad?"

"Yes," she said decisively. "But it was worth it. Oh Natalie, go down and see him." She checked the wristwatch that Jim had sent her for Christmas. "It's nursery visiting hours right now," she said. "Go down quick. You won't have any trouble picking him out. Just look for the most beautiful baby in the nursery."

My mother and I went down while Mrs. Wilkinson hovered over Eloise. The nurse brought the Foster baby to the window. I drew in my breath in a gasp. He was the worst looking baby I'd ever seen in my life. "He's all wrinkled and red and ugly," I said to my mother.

"Well, that's how they look after a long delivery," she said. "But you be sure to tell Eloise that he's beautiful."

"I'll try," I said as we went back to her room.

"Well?" Eloise beamed expectantly. "What did you think?"

"Gorgeous," I said. "Absolutely gorgeous."

Then I said to my mother, when we were well out of earshot, "I only hope he improves before Jim sees him."

Chapter 19

Another Goodbye

Dear Dolores:

Will left for overseas tonight. I went with his parents to see him off at Union Station. I am getting sick and tired of seeing the boys go off to war. It's awful, always being left behind.

I was surprised how bad I felt as I watched the train go steaming out of the station. Will and two of his buddies stood on the back deck of the train and waved their caps until they were out of sight. Both Will's parents cried and I cried too. I promised I'd write to him every day. I don't know why I said that because I know I won't. But I will try to write often.

Carl and I have become very good friends, but not boyfriend/girlfriend. Not yet anyway. He's nice enough and he's quite good-looking, (he's got wavy brown hair and a thin moustache like Clark Gable's) but people stare at you funny when you get on the streetcar with a civilian. Sometimes I feel like shouting right down the aisle, "HE'S DEAF IN ONE EAR, IF YOU MUST KNOW!"

Natalie.

The day after Will left I was late for work. I was so depressed I couldn't sleep that night. I liked my job at De Havilland and I had made quite a few new friends: Sybil Street and Marcia Donnan and a boy named Tony Myers who had flat feet.

But I began to wonder if the war would ever end. Were we going to live forever in ration-land and save stuff? Mother had special boxes lined up under the cellar stairs for salvaging: newspapers and magazines (these were saved to send the boys overseas), glass bottles, rubber bands, cans, jars of rendered fat, rags (rags went in a ragbag that hung on a nail on the wall). I wondered what on earth they would do with all that garbage. But Dad said it wasn't garbage; it would be turned into bullets and explosives and tanks and airplanes. I couldn't imagine how.

This is what I was thinking just before it happened. Sybil Street and I were working side by side, trying to get the job done before lunchtime. With glue called "dope" we were fastening strips of tape along the ribs of a Tiger Moth, the adorable little yellow planes the flyers trained on before they went overseas. I was wearing my mask, like doctors wear in the hospital, so as not to inhale the fumes from the dope, but Sybil had slipped hers down to let her upper lip dry off. She was self-conscious because she has peach fuzz, which she has to peroxide, and the sweat beads along it like a milk moustache. Well, all of a sudden she let out the weirdest groan and fell backwards. I heard a cracking noise as her head hit the cement floor. Then I saw blood trickling from under her hair and I let out a scream that could be heard all over the plant.

"HELP!" I cried. Luckily Carl was passing by and heard me. He waved both hands in the air and Morag caught the signal and came running. I whipped the bandana off my head and gave it to Carl. He wrapped it around Sybil's head.

Her face was a ghastly colour, greyish-white like newspaper, and she lay perfectly still with her eyes closed.

"WATER!" Morag screamed. One of the other girls came hurrying with a glass of water.

Morag dipped her handkerchief in the water and dribbled it on Sybil's forehead. At last her eyes flickered open. Morag lifted her head gently and put the glass to her lips.

Meantime Carl had gone for help.

"We'll get you to the hospital," Morag said soothingly. I just stood there, feeling useless as a dummy.

Two men came with a canvas stretcher. I blinked my eyes and came to life, then helped the men lift Sybil onto the stretcher. Carl tucked his sweater around her shoulders and whispered, "Don't worry, kiddo, you'll be right as rain soon." Then the men carried her away.

There was nothing to do but get back to work. I decided to go to the bathroom to bathe my face. I was feeling wretched. To reach it, you had to walk along a catwalk in full view of a room full of men working at their benches below, welding brackets with torches. It was embarrassing because everyone knew what you had to do. As I mounted the stairs, I heard whistles, and then a wave of catcalls swept the room. I stopped in my tracks, filled with anger and indignation. But then I saw Zelda Fitzpatrick, a girl with flaming red hair and freckles to match (who loves herself despite all), coming from the washroom. She was too vain to wear her overalls on her lunch break, so there she was in a short middy dress prancing along the walkway above their heads. She glanced down at them quizzically, both flustered and flattered, and then she quickened her gait. I could see her face blotched with hot pink patches as she fairly flew past, pushing me aside. I turned to tell her to watch where she was going when I saw what the hubbub was all about. The back of her dress was tucked into her white lace panties! She was gone before I could tell her. I had to laugh. To tell the truth, I wasn't all that sorry for her. She was so conceited that I had a hard time pretending to like her. I returned to my post feeling better.

At the end of the shift, Carl said, "Want a lift home, Beryl? I got the loan of my brother's car today. It's a 1938 Ford." I gratefully accepted. It was a long hike up to the plant in Downsview, and I was unnaturally tired after the horrendous events of the day. We didn't talk much on the way home. He pulled the Ford up in front of our house and turned the engine off. We sat silently for a few seconds; then all of a sudden he flung his arm across the back of my seat, lunged at me and gave me a big smackeroo right on the lips.

I didn't know what to say so I just sat there, stunned.

Carl snickered. "How about making it official?" he said, his breath steaming the car windows.

"Official?" I said.

"Sure." He gave a little snort. "Everybody at De Havilland thinks we're going steady anyhow. So...why not make it official?"

I reached for the door handle. "I don't know," I said. "I'll have to think about it."

He pulled his arm back, planted both hands on the steering wheel and stared out the steamy window. "It's because I'm in civvies isn't it?" he grumbled. "You're ashamed to be seen with a civilian."

"Oh, no," I said too quickly. "It's not that. I...I...I don't think my parents would let me. Have a boyfriend, I mean." I opened the car door. "They're old-fashioned that way." I got out as quickly as I could. "Thanks for the ride, Carl."

He didn't answer. He just leaned over and banged the door shut. Then he turned on the engine and stepped on the gas and the car skidded like a sleigh in a big circle on the icy road.

I hurried up the veranda steps and into the front hall. My mother took one look at me and cried, "Beryl! What's the matter, child?" She helped me off with my coat. "Are you sick?"

"No," I said, my voice quavering. "But there was an accident at work today." She led me into the kitchen and poured me a cup of tea from the pot that was always simmering on the Quebec Heater. After a few sips I felt better and I told her what had happened to Sybil Street.

"Morag—she's our supervisor—thinks Sybil probably has a concussion," I said. "Anyway they took her to the hospital."

Rickey looked up from the war game he was playing on the floor. "Would it be called a war wound 'cause she got hurt at war work?" he asked.

"I never thought of that," I said, "but you're probably right. She did get hurt in the line of duty."

When Dad was told about the accident he said, "Maybe you should go back to Eatons. I hear they're crying for help now."

"No," I said. "War work makes me feel patriotic. I'll just have to go to bed early so I won't fall asleep on the job. I think that's what happened to Sybil." I didn't tell him about the fumes.

I proved my point by almost falling asleep at the table over my bowl of stew. Mother had made a delicious stew from the pot roast left over from Sunday.

"We're all out of meat rations," she said, "so eat up and fortify yourselves. That's the last you'll see until next Monday."

I ate a big helping and soaked up the gravy with my daily bread ration.

Dinner perked me up so I helped with the dishes.

"There should be enough water for a warm bath," Mother said as I hung up the tea towel and staggered towards the stairs.

"Thanks," I said. But the water wasn't even lukewarm; it was cool, like the spring rain my mother catches from the downspout to rinse our hair. It woke me up, however, and I felt better so I settled, cross-legged, on my bed and opened up my diary.

March 16, 1944

Dear Dolores:

Tonight, when Carl drove me home, he asked me to be his girl. At least I think that's what he meant. Then, when I hesitated and made an excuse, he sounded mad as he said, "It's because I'm in civvies, isn't it?" And I said, no. That wasn't the reason. But…was it, Dolores? I have to admit I feel kind of embarrassed when I get on the streetcar with him. (We use the streetcars on weekends to save on gas.) People stare and whisper to each other. Sometimes they even say things right out loud, like, "My son is a Sergeant with the Princess Pats," or "My brother is a flying officer with the RCAF." And once a lady glared straight at Carl with accusing eyes. "My son is missing overseas," she said through gritted teeth.

Then I remembered how proud I was to be seen with Carmen in his airforce blue and Will in his army khakis.

But right now I've got to stop thinking about it; I've got to get my sleep so I don't have an accident at work like Sybil had today.

Goodnight, Dolores.
Natalie.

Chapter 20

Saturday, March 25, 1944

Dear Beryl,

I got your letter saying you got my "smashing news," so I know it slipped by the censors. I will get Joan to address this one, too. Maybe we can fool them one more time. Last night was the biggest operation I've been on so far. The excitement of such a mission is almost indescribable. We lumbered through the night in the company of hundreds of other aircraft, all carrying tons of bombs. Such a heavy load makes it hard to steer the aircraft and that's where a good navigator comes in handy. Our guy, Lieutenant Roy Garland, is the best damn navigator in the RAF and the same can be said for our pilot, Flying Officer Joe Hughes. In fact we consider ourselves the best damn crew in the world. After months of other bombers trying, we took out one more dam. You see, most of the time the bomb hits the water too soon and sinks harmlessly. You have to aim just right for it to hit and explode at the foot of the dam. On the way home we got caught in Jerry's searchlights, and suddenly it was up to me. I shot down a fighter plane, but not before it took potshots at us. One of our wings was badly damaged so you could say we limped home on a

wing and a prayer. The crew gave me all the credit. Damn! I am
a good gunner, if I do say so myself. (I was surprised at all those
"damns." I'd never heard Carmen swear before. But I guess
that's the way servicemen talk.)

I've got to go now, Beryl. After a mission like that we get two
days' leave. So Joan and I are going places and doing things. I'll
drop my mother a note tomorrow. Needless to say, Beryl, DON'T
show her this letter. What she doesn't know won't hurt her.

Lots of love,

Carmen.

P.S. *Joan sends her love, too.*

I thought I'd strangle on the fear that clutched my throat at
the thought of my Carmen, only nineteen years old and full
of fun—just a boy really—flying through the night in a
Lancaster Bomber. It was more than I could bear, or imagine.
I decided not to show my parents his letter this time. What
they didn't know wouldn't hurt them either.

And who was this Joan-girl to send her love to me? I was
strangely jealous of her. But I shouldn't have been. I should
have been glad that Carmen had a nice girl to be happy
with.

Chapter 21

April 16, 1944

Natalie's birthday

"Beryl…" Mother looked up from her knitting—more socks in airforce blue. She must have knitted a thousand socks by now.

"Natalie, Mother. Do I have to spell it?"

"Oh, I'll never get used to it. Anyway, Beryl or Natalie, whoever you are. What would you like to do for your birthday this year? Eighteen. I can't believe it. You're almost all grown up."

"I *am* grown up, Mother. Kids can't be war workers."

"Well…would you like a little party?"

"No. No party. There are no boys—men—worth asking."

"How about Carl Monroe? And that other boy you work with…Tony somebody?"

Dad glanced up from his paper. "What's *his* excuse?" he said.

I knew what he meant. "He's got a heart murmur," I said.

"Hmmm," Dad said. My father had been too young for the First World War and too old for the Second. So that was his excuse.

"I can't ask them both," I said to my mother. "They don't like each other."

"Well, then, I'll just make a nice Sunday dinner and we'll invite your Aunt Marie and Eloise and her parents and maybe Myra Adams and her parents. How does that sound?"

"That's okay," I answered listlessly. I had always imagined my eighteenth birthday would be a smashing big party. But the war had ruined that like everything else.

"I managed to get a nice plump chicken," My mother continued. "It's out in the woodshed keeping cold. The first thing I'm going to do when this awful war is over is buy an electric refrigerator with a little freezer on top." She nodded her head emphatically. "That's what my Victory Bonds are slated for." She rolled up her knitting. "Can you think of anyone else, Beryl?"

"Oh, I might ask Carl. But I won't ask Tony if I ask Carl because he gets really mad when Tony flirts with me. But I don't know why because I think of him more as a big brother than a boyfriend anyway."

Just then Rickey came up the cellar stairs. "You already got a big brother," he said. Standing back to back with me he stretched his neck for good measure.

"He's right," Dad said putting his hand flat on top of our heads. "He's got you beat by an inch or so already."

"He's going to be tall like his Uncle Terrence," Mom said. Uncle Terrence was my mother's half-brother. He had been posted overseas from Bagotville. He was a leading aircraftsman now. His postcards always said, "Somewhere in England."

"He's going to be a lady-killer like Uncle Terrence, too," I thought. Uncle Terrence was as handsome as the day is long. Especially in the RCAF uniform. And he had a reputation with the ladies.

Rickey's curly taffy-coloured hair fitted his head like a cap, and his big bright eyes were brown as acorns fringed with curly gold lashes. Thank goodness he's only eleven years old, I thought suddenly. Surely the war won't last another seven years.

"What did you do today, Rickey?" I asked him.

"Went to Bloor Street with Chris and Ginger," Rickey said. They were his two best friends. "We read the casualty list posted at the newsstand."

"Did...did you see the name of anybody we know?" Mother asked fearfully. Practically every boy in our neighbourhood was over there now.

"No, but Ginger did. Her cousin Randy."

"Maybe he's just missing," I said hopefully.

"His name was on the killed list," Rickey said.

"Oh, Lord," my mother said, clasping her hands prayerfully. "I hope Marie hears from Carmen again soon."

I didn't bother to ask Carl or Tony to my birthday. Eloise brought James the Third in his bassinet, and her mother and father could hardly take their eyes off him. (I must say he's improving.) Myra and her mother came over. Her father was on night duty. He's an air-raid warden. And Aunt Marie arrived with a large parcel wrapped in gold foil and tied with a silver ribbon.

"Where did you get such lovely wrapping?" my mother cried, clapping her hands.

"From the attic," Aunt Marie said. "It's pre-war paper. And you can put it in the salvage box after."

Mother had set the table in the dining room with her good china, which she hadn't used since the servicemen were here for Christmas. She thought it was unpatriotic to use good dishes when our boys in the trenches were eating off of tin plates.

It was a lovely dinner topped off with my favourite cake—orange chiffon with real orange icing flecked with rind. Where my mother got fresh oranges in April I'll never know. But it was delicious.

Eighteen white candles circled the cake and I managed to blow them all out with one huge puff.

Then they all sang "Happy Birthday."

"What did you wish for, Beryl?" Rickey asked.

"I wished that you'd call me Natalie," I said.

"Well, you wasted your wish," Rickey said.

"Oh, I was just kidding. Actually, I wished the war would be over soon."

"Well, I hope it lasts till I grow up," he said.

"Don't say that anymore, Rickey," I snapped at him.

"Why?"

"Because Mother doesn't want to hear it. Isn't it bad enough that Uncle Terrence is over there? And Cousin Carmen, and all the other boys we know?"

After supper Dad burst into song: "Leave the dishes in the sink, Ma, leave the dishes in the sink. Each dirty plate will have to wait, tonight we're going to celebrate, so leave the dishes in the sink!"

Rickey got up and went down the cellar to work on his model airplane—a torpedo bomber. Dad got him the kit for his eleventh birthday and they were building it together.

Then we all went into the front room and Dad lit the gas fireplace.

"Do you think we should be wasting gas?" Mother said.

"Well, it's a special occasion," Dad said. "Natalie's eighteenth birthday." He grinned at me as he said my name.

I opened my presents one by one: a new spring coat and matching hat from my parents. Much needed.

"I hope you like them," my mother said.

"They're swell," I said.

A blue silk scarf from Eloise to go with the coat. A pair of kid gloves from Myra and her mother. I thanked them all with as much enthusiasm as I could muster.

I had kept Aunt Marie's big gold present until last. I ripped it open because I knew the paper was destined for the salvage box under the stairs.

"Oh, Aunt Marie!" I lifted out of the box a beautiful

smoked-glass bed lamp, the kind that hooks onto the head-board and shines over your shoulder.

"I know you like to read and write in bed, Beryl, so I thought this would save you jumping up and down to reach the wall switch." Then she added, "There's another little gift in there somewhere."

I rummaged through tissue paper and came up with a flat box with a picture of the tower of London on it. I lifted the lid and inside was a note. "Birthday greetings from London, Beryl. Here's some stationery to write me letters on. From your favourite cousin, Carmen." At the corner of each page a disembodied hand was making the V for Victory sign.

"Thanks, Aunt Marie," I said, trying to swallow the lump in my throat. "Thanks, everybody."

Then Eloise said, "Well, I've got to get wee Jamie home. He's getting fussy."

One by one they left and I thanked my mother and dad for a nice birthday party.

"Maybe next year things will be different," Dad said. I knew what he meant, of course. Maybe the war would be over.

I kissed my parents goodnight and went up to my room.

Hooking my new lamp onto the headboard of my bed, I propped the writing-table with the short legs, which Dad had made me, across my knees and wrote Carmen a note on the stationery he'd sent. I told him about my birthday party and what I got for presents. I told him about my work at De

Havilland. Then I begged him to be careful. (Was that possible, I wondered, hurtling through the night in a Lancaster Bomber over Germany?) I told him to give my best wishes to Joan, too. I couldn't bring myself to send her my love. I signed and sealed the letter, and then I opened my diary.

Sunday, April 16, 1944

Dear Dolores:

Today is my eighteenth birthday. When I was young I always dreamed I'd have a big party when I turned eighteen. It's such a magic age. Eighteen! But today's party was a far cry from my dreams. There were only ten of us, counting James Foster the Third and myself.

Last year when I was seventeen I had seventeen guests, not counting my own family. The year before that, when I was sixteen, I had sixteen guests. There was Will, of course, and Rachel with her boyfriend Derrick Crisp. And the Lambert boys (triplets) and the Morrow brothers and all my girlfriends and Eloise and Jim. They had just started going steady then. And Myra and two other boys whose names I have sadly forgotten. All the boys I have listed above are overseas now. Two of them were killed in a London air raid. One is lost at sea. Oh, Dolores, will this terrible war ever end? Will life ever be normal again? Just last week Myra, two other girls and I went down to Union Station to see Aaron Vale and Cedric Foxcroft off. I wish I was a man, I really do. I think it's worse always being one of the girls waving goodbye. I'd rather be waving my wedge cap out the train window. Carmen's cap is still hanging on the back of my door. I gave my mother orders never to take it down. There it stays, I said, until he comes marching or flying home again.

Goodnight, Dolores.
Natalie.

Chapter 22

Promotion

Sybil Street was transferred into the plant office after her accident.

"I'd far rather work in the factory than the office," she said with a wistful sigh. We only got together at lunch time now.

"I wouldn't mind working in the office," I said by way of encouragement, "but I can't type fast enough."

"I'm not typing," she said. "I'm filing, and it's the most boring job in the world."

She took a bite of her honey sandwich. "How's the new girl doing?" she asked.

"Mildred Filey? Oh, she's okay."

I could tell Sybil was jealous of Mildred getting her job, so I changed the subject.

"Have you heard from your boyfriend lately?" I knew she had promised to wait for Edmund Sykes when he went overseas in January.

"Oh, I heard from him all right," she said bitterly. "He wasn't over there two months when he got engaged to a Glasgow girl."

I changed the subject again and we talked about rationing and how sick of it we were and how we wished we could buy silk stockings. Then the bell rang for the end of the lunch hour and we hurried back to our respective jobs.

It was late in the month of May and I was a real pro at my job now. And I loved every minute of it. As each new Mosquito rolled off the assembly line and out the hangar doors I wanted to jump right into the cockpit and fly it across the ocean straight to Carmen.

One day Morag came into the room and motioned to me to take off my mask, and follow her.

"The boss wants to see you, Natalie!" she shouted over the clatter.

I always thought of Morag, who was my immediate supervisor, or Carl, who was above her, as my bosses, so I didn't know whom she meant.

"Who wants to see me...Carl?" I asked.

"Nope," she said. "The big guy asked to see you."

I had only seen the "big guy" a few times as he strolled through the plant with visiting dignitaries. Once our Premier, the Honourable Mitchell Hepburn, had toured our plant. That was a thrill. But I didn't think for a minute that the big guy even knew I existed, never mind would want to see me.

"What's his name?" I asked her.

"Morris Appleby. How do you like them apples?" she joked and that lightened the mood a bit.

My knees shook as I made my way the full length of the plant. But before I got to Mr. Appleby's office I went to the washroom and took off my kerchief. I gave my hair a quick run-through with my comb and applied a bit of Tangee. I still heeded my mother's advice—*Not too much lipstick, Beryl. You don't want to look cheap.* I pinched my cheeks for colour, then went and knocked on his door.

I almost bruised my knuckles on the thick steel door before I finally heard him shout, "COME IN!"

Everyone shouted in the plant to be heard over the constant noise. I stepped inside and closed the heavy metal door behind me, shutting out the din. Then I stood with my back to the door, waiting.

I had only ever seen Mr. Appleby at a distance. So, when he stood up behind his desk he seemed to grow into a giant. He must have been six feet seven if he was an inch, with broad shoulders and a massive head full of unruly black hair.

"Sit!" he barked in a huge voice to match his head. He pointed to a big cracked leather chair facing his desk.

I sat.

The phone rang right at that moment, which gave me a chance to catch my breath and glance around the room. His office, especially his huge desk, was hidden under a mountain of paper. Rummaging through it, he managed to find the telephone cord. Then he pulled on the cord until a black cradle phone came slithering out from under the papers, scattering some of them on the floor.

The disarray of his office would make you think that the big guy was hopelessly disorganized. Yet his reputation was completely opposite; it was well known that De Havilland Aircraft ran like clockwork under Appleby's command.

He hung up the phone with a sharp clank then looked at me with the darkest eyes I had ever seen in my life. So dark that the pupils seemed drowned in them. Will had brown eyes. Mud-puddle brown. I don't know why I thought of Will's eyes right then.

Mr. Appleby didn't speak for a long moment and I thought that maybe he had expected somebody else. And I began to hope that was true.

He was studying a paper in his hand. "It says here your name is Natalie Brigham."

I didn't answer instantly. I remembered Myra's warning about using a false name and I began to wonder if this was the time to confess.

"Well..." he said gruffly. "Are you Natalie Brigham or aren't you?"

"Yes, sir," I managed to say.

"Hmmm," he muttered. "Nice name."

"Thank you, sir." I decided to keep it.

"It says here you're just eighteen."

"I'm in my nineteenth year," I said, forgetting that the paper he held in his hand had my birthdate right on it.

His lips twitched. "I told Carl Monroe I thought you were too young for the job," he said.

"What job…sir?" I felt like I was in deep water.

"Why, Morag Parsons job, of course. Didn't they tell you?"

"Morag's job? Is she leaving?"

"Yes. It seems that Morag has decided to add to the burden of the human race."

If it weren't for Eloise's baby, I thought, I wouldn't have known what in the world he was talking about.

Morag's husband was away in the navy.

"Terrible world to bring an innocent child into," he muttered as if to himself.

"Oh, I don't know." I surprised myself by answering because I don't think he was talking to me. "My dad says the war will be over soon and Toronto will become a boom town just like it did after the last war."

He frowned and contemplated. Then he said, "Well…do you think you can handle it? Morag's job?"

I frowned too. "I think I could handle it," I said.

"But—"

"But what?" His voice got a bit edgy.

"There are older women out there who might not like it," I said.

"Well, Carl Monroe and Morag Parsons have both recommended you in spite of your age." He shook his huge head as if he could hardly agree less. "So, the job's yours if you want it. Make up your mind. I haven't got all day."

I hesitated for one more second—a split second. "I'll take it," I said.

He stood up then and so did I. Towering over me like a veritable giant, he leaned across his messy desk and shook my hand so hard my fingers cracked.

Morag and I spent the next few hours with our heads together. Some of the other girls—they were all called girls but some were as old as my mother—eyed us suspiciously.

By the time I got home that night I was flying high as a Mosquito. I could hardly wait to get my coat off to rush into the kitchen to tell my parents. I was late getting home so they had already started supper.

Chapter 23

Letter from Carmen

But before I had a chance to say a word, Rickey said, "There's a big thick letter come for you, Beryl. We think it's from Carmen 'cause that girl's handwriting is on the envelope again."

It had been weeks since I had had a letter from Carmen. And Aunt Marie had had only one postcard. The picture on the postcard showed a little boy in full army uniform saluting, and the caption under it read, Come on Canada, Britain needs you now! But Carmen's words on the postcard had been censored so it didn't tell us much.

I ate my supper in five minutes flat and took the letter up to my room.

"Why don't you read it to us?" complained Rickey.

"I will in a minute," I said.

Shutting my bedroom door I turned on my bed lamp. The letter was in a white civilian envelope. I opened it with shaky fingers; there were four full pages, uncensored.

Sunday, May 14, 1944

Hi, Beryl! Or should I say Natalie? Joan, my girlfriend, likes your new name better. I liked her better immediately.

Well, have I got news for you! Last night all our intensive training paid off. The big raid took place at 0900 hours. Our target dams were the Mohne, the Eder and the Sorpe. We were required to drop our bombs from a perfectly level flying position exactly sixty feet above the lake just back of the dam. I don't think this will make much sense to you so I'll draw a little sketch to try to make it clearer.

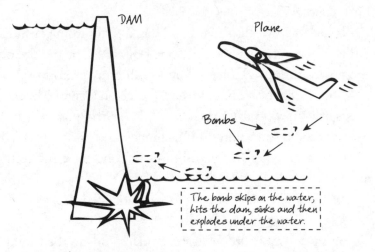

The bomb skips on the water, hits the dam, sinks and then explodes under the water.

The bomb skipped along the surface (like skipping stones on Lake Ontario) until it hit the dam. Then it sank to a predetermined depth and exploded, cracking the dam wide open. Tons of water went rushing through the huge hole, flooding the powerhouse and overflowing the river. It destroyed factories and homes and everything in its wake, drowning about 1,500 Germans. I shuddered at the thought.

Two of the three dams were completely demolished, but the Sorpe sustained only minor damage. We'll get it next time!

Only we Dambusters were involved in this raid and we had no fighter protection. It was a round trip and the fighter planes could not carry enough fuel to go with us. So we were on our own. We lost forty-nine men on that raid. Our squadron consisted of twenty aircraft so you can see that we sustained heavy losses. There are usually seven men in a Lancaster crew, but in ours there were eight—one extra gunner in the nose of the aircraft to man the machine guns. And that extra gunner was yours truly!

The raid, in spite of our terrible losses, was considered an overwhelming success because it knocked out so many German war-plants and left them without electricity and manpower.

Our tour of duty consists of thirty such missions and after that we get a two-week leave. Joan and I are hoping to find a peaceful spot here in England where we can forget all about the war for two whole weeks.

Well, Bery—oops, Natalie—that's about all I have to say this time. I hope it won't worry you too much. We Damnbusters are a close-knit squadron, and we figure that as long as we stick together, we'll all make it home.

I don't need to tell you not to show this letter to my mother. I'd rather your parents didn't read it either so try to keep it to yourself.

Joan sends her love.

> *Your favourite cousin,*
> *Carmen.*

When I went back downstairs, they were all waiting with baited breath to hear Carmen's letter.

"He...he asked me not to show it to anybody," I had to tell them.

"Well, why not?" My mother wore a worried frown.

"Aren't you going to show it to *his* mother?" Dad asked.

"No," I said. "It's top secret and the fewer people who know what's going on the better. That's what Carmen said."

"How did it pass the censors if it's top secret?" my dad asked.

"He had a friend send it in a civilian envelope," I said.

"I don't like the sound of that," Dad said.

"I'll tell Aunt Marie if you don't show us," threatened Rickey.

"No, you won't," my mother said. "She's worried enough already."

"I've got other news," I said.

"What other news?" They didn't sound very interested. And after reading Carmen's letter, I had lost interest in my new job myself.

"I got a promotion at the plant," I said. "I've been made a forelady. And I'm getting a ten dollar a week raise. That is, if I do a good job."

"Well, then, with the extra money you can buy more Victory Bonds," Dad said. "That's the least we can do to help win this war."

Chapter 24

June 6, 1944, D-Day

My new job kept my mind off the war news until D-Day.

You couldn't miss it. It was spread all over the papers in huge black headlines. BRITISH AND CANADIAN TROOPS LAND ON JUNO AND GOLD BEACH. AMERICAN TROOPS LAND ON OMAHA BEACH.

That night we were glued to the radio. Lorne Greene, our Toronto broadcaster, gave us the awesome details. "There are many casualties on both sides," he said in his deep and sombre voice. "But under General Dwight D. Eisenhower, victory is assured."

We didn't talk; we just listened. Eloise and her parents came in to listen with us. It made it more bearable, somehow, to be huddled together around the radio.

It wasn't until we read the casualty lists in the paper the next day that we found out Private James Foster was safe. And that Private Will Ashby had been killed. The shock of seeing Will's name left me senseless. I didn't really believe it until I went up the street that night to see his parents. It was the hardest thing I ever had to do. Nothing I said helped. Will's parents were inconsolable.

Aunt Marie was beside herself. None of us had heard a word from Carmen in weeks.

"No news is good news," my mother insisted.

"Carmen's squadron wouldn't be involved in the invasion, Marie," Dad said. "So I'm sure he is safe and sound."

Two weeks later we finally saw some footage of the actual landings in the movie theatres. The lineup at the College Theatre was a block long.

They always showed the news first before the movie. I strained my eyes to see if I could recognize Will lying dead on the beach or floating in the water. But of course they all looked alike from the air.

Carl and I had gone to see *The Wings of Wrath* but I just couldn't sit through it after watching the real thing.

"What good will it do to miss the movie?" Carl sounded disgruntled as we left halfway through. And at that moment I knew I wouldn't go to see a war film with a civvy ever again. How deaf could he be, I thought, if he could hear everything that was said in the newsreel?

Chapter 25

Saturday afternoon

I heard the screams half a block away right through the storm door. It was Aunt Marie and she was waving a telegram above her head.

I snatched the yellow paper out of her hand and pulled her in the door. She was shaking from head to toe as if she had the palsy. I led her through the hall and sat her down in the easy chair.

My fingers shook so badly I could hardly read the dreaded words: *We regret to inform you that your son, Sergeant Carmen Alan Baker and crew of Squadron 617 are reported missing in action. The Lancaster Bomber, flight 999, failed to return from its mission. Further details will follow. Lieutenant Donald South, OHMS.*

My mother came in from shopping. The minute she saw Aunt Marie, she dropped two bags of groceries on the floor. I heard the eggs smash.

I handed her the telegram over Aunt Marie's head. Aunt Marie had not stopped sobbing. Her trim little body vibrated like a twanging wire in my arms.

As she read, my mother's face drained of colour. "Oh, Marie," she murmured. "Oh, Marie. Oh, Marie." Then she said, "Beryl, call the doctor."

The minute Dad saw the doctor's car parked in front of our house he knew what had happened.

Dr. Braden gave Aunt Marie a needle in her arm, and mother took her upstairs and loosened her clothes. She went to sleep almost instantly.

Dr. Braden left white pills and said to give them to her every few hours. Snapping his bag shut with a worried frown he said, "She shouldn't be left alone. Can she stay here for now?"

"Of course," my mother said, her voice just above a whisper.

Dr. Braden had been our family physician for as long as I could remember. He had delivered Carmen and Cary (Carmen's twin who died) and me and Rickey, too.

We walked with him to the front door. "She'll sleep for two or three hours," he said, his hand on the doorknob. "I'll call again tomorrow."

"Thank you, Doctor." Mother went straight back up stairs.

I made tea in the kitchen. When she came back down we sat around the kitchen table, sipping our tea, not talking.

Finally, Rickey broke the silence. "Is Carmen dead for sure?" he said in an awed whisper.

"No," Dad said. "Missing means just that. Missing. When they find the plane they'll know."

"Oh," my mother lamented. "If only Carmen wasn't her only child. If only…"

"Mother!" My voice cracked like a whiplash. "Do you really think it would hurt her less if she had another kid? Is a mother's love divided up in slices like pieces of pie?" I was ashamed the minute the cruel words were out of my mouth. It was as if I had slapped her face.

Then Dad said in a muffled voice, "Beryl's right you know, Jean. It wouldn't make a particle of difference." Mother didn't respond, so Dad said, "When my mother got the telegram about Robert," (Robert was his oldest brother who had been killed in the dying days of World War One) "my sister and I both knew that we could never make it up to her."

We took turns going upstairs to look in on Aunt Marie. While she slept we ate a bite of supper, then turned the radio on low and listened to Jim Hunter's six o'clock newscast. Of course no mention was made of the missing aircraft. And who knew how many others had not returned? I remembered that in Carmen's last letter he had said that in one mission they had lost fifty-nine men.

When the news was over Dad turned off the radio. To keep our spirits up, we usually listened to "The Story Hour," which came on every night right after the news. The stories about great heroism under fire were always uplifting. But in the stories, miracles happened—the planes always made it safely back to home base, the soldiers always lived to tell the tale because they had only sustained flesh wounds, and the sailors always got rescued at sea by patrolling corvettes.

But the telegram was real. This was not a story with an automatic happy ending.

Mother got Aunt Marie to take a little soup and another pill, then we tucked her into my bed. I took my things—my nightgown and slippers and Pond's cold cream and my black bobby pins that matched my hair (as if it mattered)—and went downstairs.

Dad had the davenport made up for me. Then he put his hat and coat on (it had turned cold and had begun to snow) and went over to Aunt Marie's house on Dufferin Street to feed the cats and let them out and lock the doors.

When the house was all quiet for the night, like the western front, I propped myself up on two pillows and pulled the chain on my bed lamp. Then I opened my diary on my knees.

Oct. 21, 1944

Oh, Dolores, (I began in shaky handwriting). I think the worst has happened. But I mustn't let myself believe it. We have to be strong for Aunt Marie's sake. But, no, not just for her sake. For my own, too. Because I have a strange confession to make, and I can only make it to you, Dolores. I think I am in love with Carmen. Now, I know he's my cousin, my second cousin, or, as my mother would put it, once removed. But I don't honestly think that matters anymore. In fact I'm pretty sure King George and Queen Mary (the old King and Queen I'm talking about) were first cousins. That's what I heard anyway.

Dr. Braden gave us all a little pill to calm us down. I think I'll take mine now and try to go to sleep.

Sadly,
Natalie.

Aunt Marie stayed for three days. Mother took her meals up on a tray but they came back down almost untouched. Mostly Aunt Marie just took the pills and slept. Then one night after supper, she came downstairs all dressed in her hat and coat, pulling on her gloves.

"I'm going home," she announced.

"You don't want to be alone yet," my mother said.

"I have to be near my telephone."

"Then I'll come with you."

Aunt Marie didn't object, so Mother got her outdoor clothes on, took hold of her aunt's arm, and went home with her.

When she returned that night about ten o'clock, Mother said, "She wants to be alone. I'm worried about her."

Chapter 26

No News Is Good News?

Weeks went by, then months, and still no word from Carmen.

The war continued to dominate our lives.

Aunt Marie stopped going out altogether, so Mother went over to her house every day. She shopped for her and cooked for her and made sure everything was clean and tidy.

In our house you'd never know it was only two weeks before Christmas. There were no preparations whatsoever. Usually the house was filled with wonderful baking aromas— bubbling mincemeat pies and steaming plum puddings and the spicy smell of gingerbread men. And the cardboard box of decorations would be spilled out on the living-room floor in front of the Christmas tree. But this year there wasn't a sign of Christmas.

Then one night, just days before Christmas, Dad came in from his Civil Defence duties, took off his helmet and armband and hung up his coat in the front hall.

Mother and I were sitting at the table listlessly drinking tea.

"What's for supper?" Dad said coming into the kitchen.

"Oh, Jack, I'm sorry," Mother said, running her fingers distractedly through her hair. "I haven't had time to think about it and Beryl has just got home this minute and…"

Dad poured himself a cup of tea and sat down opposite Mother. "Listen, Jean," he said in a quiet but firm voice, "this has got to stop. If you keep waiting on Marie hand and foot she'll be an invalid by the time Carmen comes home. She's got to start doing for herself."

"I know. I'm worn to a frazzle running back and forth. But what else can I do?"

"You'll have to talk to her about it because if you keep it up, you'll make yourself sick, and Marie will never set foot outdoors again."

But he was wrong. The very next night Aunt Marie could be heard screaming all over the neighbourhood. We flung open the door just as she came running up our walk waving another telegram.

"Maybe it's good news this time," cried Rickey hopefully.

But one look at Aunt Marie's stricken face told us otherwise.

The telegram read, *We regret to inform you that your son, Sergeant Carmen Alan Baker is now missing, presumed dead.*

The world collapsed around us. I gave up my room to Aunt Marie again and settled myself on the davenport for the duration.

Completely drained of feelings, I got out my diary and wrote,

Dear Dolores:

This will be my last letter to you. Carmen is dead. I took his cap off my bedroom door and put it in the shoebox where I keep his letters and postcards. I have decided not to harbour false hopes. Well, Dolores, you've been a good friend. I don't know what I would have done without you. But this is goodbye.

Sincerely,
Natalie.

Chapter 27

New Year's, 1945

On New Year's Day, Aunt Marie once again surprised us and went home. She gave no explanation, she just packed up her things and left.

"I'll come over bright and early tomorrow, Marie!" Mother called after her as she went trailing up the street through the snow.

"Thank you, Jean. That'll be nice," Aunt Marie called back. Then she disappeared around the corner of College Street. Dad threw his coat on and followed her. He had kept her home fires burning and had looked after her cats while she stayed with us. So when she shut her front door behind her, he knew she was safe and warm, and he came back.

I never missed a day's work. The plant was on full wartime footing, so we had to hire a batch of new girls. And it was my job to teach them to work on Mosquitoes. The little fighter planes were still in great demand. Sometimes we had to fill an order for 100 planes, and as fast as we built them, they disappeared across the ocean and another order would come in for hundreds more. Once we got ahead of ourselves and ran out of storage space. So Carl and his crew had to haul them up on pulleys to the ceiling.

One of the crew, a middle-aged man with a limp, was our poet laureate. He gave me a copy of his latest verse:

The ships come pouring off the line
At such a dizzy pace,
And then go soaring for a time
Until they take their place
Beside the incompletes,
That hang from up above,
Awaiting wings, and other things,
That all good airmen love.
For without motors, wings and tails,
They cannot turn and dive.
Let's hope that they can hit the trail
By nineteen forty-five.

"Anybody want to go to the show after work?" asked Sharon. She was one of my new girls I was teaching to paste the wings.

"What's playing?" asked Marion Fellows.

"Well, there's *Captains of the Clouds*, starring James Cagney and Dennis Morgan," Sharon said, scanning the newspaper while we ate our lunch.

"I don't want to see that," I said. It was obvious by the title that it was an airforce story. I never wanted to see another airplane explode in the sky, even if it was a German Messerschmitt.

"Let's try to find a love story then," Marion said, skimming the show page. "This sounds good. *Hold Back The Dawn*, starring Charles Boyer and Paulette Goddard."

"I love Boyer's French accent," put in Sharon.

"It looks more like a love story than a war story anyway," I said.

So that's what we did to keep our minds off the war. We went to movies on weeknights, if we didn't have to work overtime, and on the weekends we went to dances at the Armouries. That was the only place where there were any men left to dance with. And they were always just passing through on their way overseas or to some army training station.

By the time March came and you could smell spring in the air, we had seen just about every movie ever made. The theatres even brought back Laurel and Hardy and Our Gang Comedies to lighten the mood of the times.

I had worked all day Saturday, March tenth, and had put in three hours overtime. So by the time I staggered in our front door I was half-asleep on my feet.

"Oh, Beryl. You look done in," my mother said, concerned. "But just look what you've got in the mail."

She handed me a letter, and the girlish handwriting gave me a turn. It was the same handwriting that had been on all of Carmen's letters. It was Joan's, his girlfriend's, writing. Was it from him? Could it be? I dared to hope for a second, but then hope died when I realized that if he had been found alive Aunt Marie would have been the first to hear.

I ripped open the letter and unfolded two pages of cramped writing—Joan's writing, not Carmen's—on both sides.

Chapter 28

Letters from Joan

120 Victoria Street,
Hendon, England,
Feb. 3, 1945.

Dear Beryl,

I hope you will forgive me for writing to you. But you are my only connection with Carmen, and of course you know why I have your address at my fingertips. I am the girl who addressed his letters to you so they would look 'civilian.'

If you have any news of Carmen I beg you to write and tell me. Even if it is bad. I cannot find anything out from the War Department here because I am not actually related to him in any way. All I know for sure is that his aircraft never returned from its last mission. I did not know any of the rest of the crew, even though half of them were English and half Canadian.

Can you tell me anything, Beryl? I will be grateful for any bit of news. I know that you were Carmen's favourite cousin and you came second only to his mother in his thoughts and affections. I will wait for your answer anxiously.

Your sincere friend,
Joan Summerville.

I reread the letter. As I did so, unexpected waves of jealousy washed over me. This Joan-person was the last one to see Carmen. She had probably kissed him goodbye. I wondered how close they had become. Were they lovers? Were they thinking of getting married? That happened so often nowadays. Only last week both Katie Parr and Sybil Street got what were commonly called "Dear Joan" letters. The letters were from boyfriends and even fiancés, telling the girls they left behind that they had fallen in love with someone over there and were about to get married. Or were already married. It struck me as ironic that these letters were called "Dear Joan" letters. And my letter was from Joan.

I knew that I shouldn't be feeling this way about Carmen. After all, we were cousins and we had never had a romance—nothing like that. We had been practically brought up together. We had been in and out of each other's houses all our childhood. Why, I remembered that when Carmen was only a toddler himself (I was ten months younger than he was), he tried to teach me how to walk. He walked backwards, holding both my hands and saying, "C'mon, Beryly. C'mon Beryly!" Yet his kiss goodbye at Union Station still lingered on my lips. "Don't worry, kiddo." I could still hear his voice, clear as crystal, in my mind. "I'll be back as soon as I blast Jerry right off the map."

"What is it, Beryl?"

I handed my mother the letter. She read it and handed it back to me with a sigh. "I guess you'd better tell her," she said.

"Tell her what?"

"What we know. Tell her what was in both telegrams."

"Shouldn't I have Aunt Marie's permission to do that?" I asked defensively. "She's never even heard of this Joan-person."

"Then I think it's time she did. Maybe 'this Joan-person,' as you put it, could tell Carmen's mother things she'd like to know."

That night I resurrected my diary and poured my heart out to Dolores. *I am very mixed up wondering what to do, Dolores,* I wrote. *If only you could answer me.*

Then, almost mystically, the next words appeared on the page: *Dear Natalie, Yes, write to Joan and tell her all you know. Ask her about her friendship (relationship?) with Carmen. Don't tell your Aunt until you have more information. It's up to you to find out if what this girl has to say will be good news for his mother, or bad. You be the judge, Natalie. Sincerely, Dolores.*

Out of the shoebox—where I kept Carmen's letters and postcards, his airforce cap and the brooch he'd given me the night before he left (the brooch was RCAF silver wings and I was afraid to wear it because the clasp was uncertain and I was afraid I might lose it)—I got the stationery pad and matching envelopes he'd sent me for Christmas.

332 Gladstone Avenue,
Toronto, Ontario.
February 17, 1945.

Dear Joan:

I received your letter today. All I can tell you is that Aunt Marie, Carmen's mother, has had two telegrams from the War Department. The first one said, "We regret to inform you that the crew of the Lancaster Bomber, squadron 617, has failed to return from its last mission."

Then, some weeks later, another telegram arrived, saying that the whole crew was missing, presumed dead.

Until I hear from you again I will not tell Carmen's mother anything. In fact, she has never seen the letters that you mailed for Carmen and that came to me uncensored. We, my mother and father and myself, decided that, because the missions he described were so horrendously dangerous, (he even drew diagrams of the action) it would be better if she did not know such frightening details. Carmen is her only child and she dotes on his every word. The letters and postcards he sent to her were always cheerful and fun filled, and gave no hint of the true nature of his missions.

I'm glad you told me that I was second only to his mother in his affections. We were kindred spirits, Carmen and I.

I can't tell you any more right now. I will look forward to hearing from you again. Please tell me everything that you can. Everything.

Your friend,
Natalie Brigham (nee Beryl).

Two weeks later Joan's second letter arrived.

Hendon, England,
Feb. 28, 1945.

Dear Natalie:

I was so glad to get your letter but I am heartbroken at the news. Yet it only confirms my suspicions. There is so much death and destruction here in Britain that you'd almost think we'd get used to such bad news. But, no, the heartaches never stop.

I will tell you a little bit about myself. I live in Hendon, which is a small place about twenty miles west of London. My family consists of my mother, father and my little sister, Jocelyn. Carmen came to our house several times and my family liked him very much. Jocelyn loved his Canadian accent.

In Hendon there is an airbase where the RAF trains its new recruits. On Saturday nights there is always a dance in the Canteen, and that's where I met Carmen. I remember the song that was playing on the record player. Kate Smith (the American lady with the big voice) was singing "He wears a pair of silver wings," and Carmen came up to me shyly and said, "I'm not a very good dancer, but would you care to take a chance?" And that was it! I fell for him head over heels. After that I didn't bother seeing any other boys. I was sure he was the one for me.

A wave of jealousy spread over me. So they were in love!

I knew, of course, that his missions were incredibly dangerous, but he always made me believe by his positive thinking that he was the best "damn" gunner in the RAF, and that the Dambusters were the best "damn" airmen in the world. "Damn" was the only swear word I ever heard Carmen use, and it helped to convince me that the Dambusters were, indeed, invincible.

He was due for a week's leave after that last mission and we were going to go to the seaside together. I hope that does not shock you too much. We had not talked about marriage yet but I was HOPING. It was my dream to come to Canada as a war bride. But I would not marry him just to get a ticket to Canada. Please believe that, Natalie. ("Beryl" was scratched out.) *I truly loved (I truly love) your cousin. If we were married I'd be your cousin, too, wouldn't I?* (I must tell her in my next letter that Carmen and I are cousins twice removed, I thought.) *Maybe, by a miracle, this will still happen. I looked up the word "presume" in my Oxford and it says, "Presume: take for granted on probable grounds." Now that sounds like it's not for sure, doesn't it? We cannot give up hope can we? Please write again soon.*

Your good friend,
Joan.

Chapter 29

Two more letters passed between us before I decided to tell Aunt Marie about Joan.

Mother was sure it was the right thing to do. Dad was not so sure.

He was pulling the blackout curtains needlessly, I thought, across the front-room windows and settling them on the sill. "It will only get her hopes up," he said in a morose voice.

"But we can't give up hope, Dad." I answered him sharply.

"We have to be realistic," he said.

"Marie has a right to know what's in those letters," Mother insisted. "And you haven't been over to see her lately, Beryl. She'll be glad of your company."

With an elastic band from the box that Mother was saving as part of the war effort, I snapped the sheaf of letters together, tucked them in the pocket of my shortie coat, tied a kerchief over my head (it had been a mild day for mid-April but wet) and walked over to Aunt Marie's house on Dufferin Street.

The house, an ordinary house much like ours on Gladstone Avenue, seemed too big for one little wisp of a woman to live in all alone.

She answered my knock almost instantly, and I was struck by how thin and tiny she was. She actually seemed to be shrinking. "Oh, Beryl. It's lovely to see you. I hope you've got time for a cup of tea. I just got my sugar rations today so I baked a cake for something to do."

I kicked off my rubbers, hung up my coat on the wall rack, and followed my aunt down the hall. The hall led through the dining room, where Aunt Marie's upright piano stood by the window. I was startled to see Carmen's picture in a large frame on top of the piano, spotlighted with a gooseneck lamp. I remembered the day I had gone with him, down Yonge Street, to the Paramount Studios. Two other servicemen, sailors, had been there to get their portraits taken. Carmen had given the picture to his mother for her birthday and she had hand tinted it herself. She was very good at tinting. She got the colour of his blue eyes and reddish-brown hair just right.

The sight of him in his airforce blue uniform—his cap at a jaunty angle, his silver wings shining on his breast, his smile bursting with life—nearly made my legs give way. I averted my gaze and hurried after Aunt Marie into the kitchen; his painted blue eyes seemed to follow me.

"The tea's ready. I was just about to have some," she said. Then she noticed the envelopes in my hand. "What have you got there, Beryl?" she asked.

There was a little ray of hope in her eyes and I wondered if Dad was right. What good would it do to give her false hope? But, as Mother said, maybe she needed to know that there was a girl in England who loved her son.

I told her briefly about how I came to hear from Joan. I decided not to mention Carmen's letters to me. I only hoped that she wouldn't ask to see them.

I sipped my tea and nibbled at the piece of cake as Aunt Marie read Joan's letters.

She read them one by one, her lips moving silently; then she read them over again. She never once looked up but I saw tears, like rivulets, wending down the long lines in her cheeks from the corners of her eyes to the corners of her mouth. After reading them twice, she slipped them back into the envelopes and put them on the table. Then she mopped her face with her apron. She didn't speak for what seemed like a long time. Finally she said, "He's only nineteen. That's far too young to marry."

My heart flopped. Oh, Lord, I thought, was Dad right? Had the letters given her false hopes? I didn't know what to say so I said nothing.

"Of course in wartime..." she continued quietly, "...things are different, aren't they?" She frowned thoughtfully. "But I wouldn't mind, really, if she was a nice girl.... She sounds like a nice girl, doesn't she, Beryl?"

"Yes," I managed to answer in spite of the lump in my throat. Should I tell her that it would take a miracle? Should

I remind her, gently, of the two telegrams?

She reached out and plucked the padded tea cosy off the pot and filled our cups again. I helped myself to cream and sugar. We had run out of sugar days ago, so I couldn't resist the temptation to scoop up two teaspoonfuls. Then I stirred it quietly around in the pretty teacup. I ate two pieces of cake and I noticed that Aunt Marie didn't even touch it.

The kitchen clock ticked off the seconds. Five minutes passed. I was trying to think of something to say. Perhaps I should say I have to go home now because I have to wash my hair and get ready for work tomorrow.

"They could stay here with me until they got on their feet," Aunt Marie said. Then she fell silent again for at least another five minutes. A shiver ran down my spine.

"Well, Aunt Marie..." my voice broke the silence. It was too loud and I lowered it almost to a whisper. "I have to be going now because I've got work tomorrow."

"I know, dear." She picked up the letters and handed them back to me. "I'll walk you to the door."

I sat on the hall bench and pulled on my rubbers. She got my coat from the rack and held it open for me. Then she buttoned me up and tied the kerchief under my chin as if I was a child. I noticed I was much taller than she was now.

With my hand on the door latch I said, "Mother said to tell you she'll be over tomorrow." Mother hadn't actually said anything, but I knew she would be. I opened the door a crack and cold air knifed in.

Suddenly she reached up, placed both hands on my cheeks, and turned my head towards her. "It's all right, Beryl," she said. "I understand, I really do. I'm just dreaming. There's no harm in dreaming, is there?"

"No, Aunt Marie. I do a lot of dreaming myself."

When I got to the sidewalk I turned to see if she'd gone in. The door was shut and the hall light was turned off.

She knows, I thought. Mother was right about the letters.

Chapter 30

Jim's Homecoming

Private James Foster came home for good on the last day of March. He had been wounded in action and he had to go straight to Christie Street Hospital. It was a special hospital for veterans. Some World War One veterans were still there, living out their days.

The news was good about Jim. The doctor assured Eloise that he would recover fully once they got the shrapnel out of his right leg.

"Oh, Beryl!" Eloise was ecstatic. "I mean, Natalie. Jim looks wonderful. Wait till you see him. Would you like to come with me on the weekend? We'll say you're his sister. You've both got jet-black hair, so that should fool those bossy nurses. You wouldn't believe how strict they are about visitors. And of course Jamie isn't allowed in the hospital because of germs. And the visiting hours are so short. But I'll have him home soon, thank goodness. Married couples shouldn't be apart too long, you know," she rolled her eyes meaningfully. "Of course we'll be staying with my mother and father until Jim is perfectly well. Then we'll get our own flat. Won't that be romantic? Having our own little home?"

I felt the nasty taste of jealousy in spite of myself. It came up in my throat like bile. Even though I don't think I would ever have married Will Ashby, I still felt cheated that I wouldn't have the chance because he was never coming home.

Chapter 31

As time passed, a strange void came into our lives. We stopped talking about Carmen. And strangely, some days I actually forgot about him. After the memorial service, I finally gave up and said goodbye. I didn't want to think about him anymore. Poor Aunt Marie said over and over she wanted a grave to visit, but nobody even knew where he was. "He's probably in the English Channel," Dad said. But we didn't say that to Aunt Marie.

Aunt Marie went around like a ghost. Sometimes she would slip into our kitchen, glance around, and slip back out again without speaking.

The news was full of rumours that the war was winding down, but we were afraid to believe it. The work at De Havilland had slowed up and some of the newer girls had been laid off already.

Yet, in spite of the war winding down, the casualty lists grew even longer. I couldn't bear to look anymore because too often I saw a name I recognized.

Chapter 32

WAR ENDS! GERMANY SURRENDERS!
The amazing news came blasting over the radio. We had been listening for days, hardly daring to hope for such a miracle.

All over the plant, tools clattered to the floor and everyone was screaming and laughing and hugging and kissing each other.

"NO MORE WORK TODAY!" Carl was standing on a worktable, shouting through a newspaper megaphone. Jumping down off the table, he shouted in my ear, "C'mon, Beryl, let's head downtown."

He drove at breakneck speed. I hung on to the sides of the seat with white knuckles. By the time we got to Bloor Street, the traffic was piling up. Horns were honking and people were pouring out of stores and houses, and hanging out of upstairs windows.

At last we reached Yonge Street but the cars were lined up, bumper to bumper, horns honking and the crowd roaring. What a tumult! We couldn't drive any farther. So we abandoned the car in a vacant lot and joined the cheering mob.

Flags appeared out of second-floor windows. Union Jacks and Red Ensigns waved over our heads as we went marching triumphantly towards City Hall. I never kissed so many strangers in all my life.

That night we listened on the radio to a rebroadcast of Prime Minister Winston Churchill's pronouncement from Number Ten Downing Street in London. Then the King spoke from Buckingham Palace and we could hear Big Ben tolling in the background. Next came President Truman, speaking from the White House in Washington, and last but not least, our own Prime Minister, Mackenzie King, from Ottawa, Ontario.

The next day, Wednesday, was declared a national holiday. The excitement, mixed with relief, was almost unbearable.

Mother kept trying to get Aunt Marie on the telephone.

"It just keeps ringing and ringing," she said worriedly, as she hung up the receiver. "Beryl, you stay here with Rickey and your dad, and I'll go over to check on her."

Dad was off work today too. Everybody was.

"C'mon, Rick," I said to my little brother. "Let's run up to Bloor Street to see what's going on."

"You mean it's really over...the war?" asked Rickey in a disappointed voice.

"Yes," I said as I grabbed his hand.

"Aawww!" he complained. "Now I'll never get to wear a uniform."

"Yes, you will," I said. "You can join the Boy Scouts."

"It's not the same," he grumbled breathlessly as we ran.

"That's right," I said. "And when you grow up you'll know how lucky you were."

A week later I received a package from Britain. Joan had sent me the front pages of all the newspapers the day that peace was declared. The headlines, PEACE AT LAST! were three inches deep and the pictures showed throngs of people crowded into Piccadilly Circus and Trafalgar Square and all across London Bridge.

It was much like the scenes in Toronto except for one big difference—in the background, silhouetted against the sky, were the jagged remains of bombed-out buildings.

I spread the pages out on the dining-room table for my family to see. Rickey studied the photos one by one. "I mighta got killed," he said in an awestruck whisper.

Mother was looking over his shoulder. She kissed the top of his head. "Your poor Aunt Marie," she said.

Chapter 33

Goodbye, De Havilland

Carl kept me on as long as he possibly could. But as the boys came home and changed their uniforms for civvies, we girls got fired one by one.

"It's not fair," I said to Carl the day he reluctantly gave me my pink slip and my final pay-packet. "I know the job better than any of them." I waved my hand at the men in new De Havilland overalls waiting to be told what to do. "You could at least let me show them the ropes."

Carl shook his head decisively. "That wouldn't work," he said. "They'd never stand for it."

"Stand for what?" I demanded.

"For being shown the job by a girl."

"I'm not a girl, I'm a woman," I snapped at him. "Besides, they had women teachers in school, didn't they?"

"That's different. They were kids then. They're men now. Veterans. They've got a right to the jobs."

I nearly said, How come you've got a right, then? You're not a veteran any more than I am. I never really believed his deaf-in-one-ear excuse. But I clamped my mouth shut and didn't say it.

What's the use, I thought. It's not really Carl's fault he has to lay off all the women. It's company policy. Veterans first.

"What are you going to do with yourself, Beryl?" As soon as he saw the pink slip in my hand my dad reverted back to my old, pre-war name.

"I haven't decided yet," I shrugged.

My mother stood in the kitchen doorway, a potato in one hand and paring knife in the other. "Well…" she said. "It's never too late."

"Too late for what?" I asked.

"To go back to school. You can take all summer off and go back in September."

"But…I've missed a whole year."

"You've still got your books haven't you?" asked my dad.

"Yeah."

"Then bone up over the summer and by fall you'll be all set. What form will you be in?"

"Fourth form," I said. "And I've forgotten all my third form shorthand."

"Well, then, bone up," he repeated.

"*I* gotta go to school," Rickey said, "so why not you?"

"Because you're still a kid. I'm a woman now. And working grows you up."

"Well, take your time and think it over," Dad said.

The next day I slept in until ten o'clock. It was strange to sleep in on a weekday. I got dressed lethargically, ate a late breakfast and phoned Myra. She had been fired from Dominion Bridge two weeks ago and I hadn't seen her since.

She answered the phone.

"Oh, it's only you," she yawned. She sounded as if she'd just got up too.

"What's that supposed to mean?" I said.

"Well, I put my job application in two places: Eatons and Simpson's, and I was hoping it was one of them."

"Well, it's only me. Let's go for a walk," I said. "I need to talk to somebody."

Ordinarily, I would have gone straight to Eloise if I needed a confidant, but since her marriage and motherhood—and especially now that Jim was home from the hospital—she was all tied up with her marital duties. I didn't envy her anymore. I decided I liked my freedom.

It was perfect summer weather, hot and sunny. Myra and I strolled along College Street, stopping to look at the pictures outside the College Theatre at Dovercourt Road.

"Nelson Eddy and Jeanette MacDonald in *Naughty Marietta*. I love them singing together," I said. "And what a relief from all the war stories we've had to put up with."

"Let's go tonight," Myra said.

"Okay," I said, and we continued to stroll along College Street under the dappled shade of big oak and maple trees.

"What did you want to talk to me about?" asked Myra.

"Well, my parents want me to go back to school and get my commercial diploma," I explained.

"My mother likes me paying board," Myra said. "She's already ordered an electric refrigerator. She wants me to get another job and quick."

"My mother ordered a Kelvinator," I said. "She's going to pay for it with her war bonds. So she doesn't need my board. Anyway, Eatons sent her a postcard saying it won't be available for at least six months."

"Why on earth would it take so long to get a refrigerator now that the war's over?" puzzled Myra.

"Because all the factories have to convert their machinery back from munitions to domestic," I said. "Except airplane factories like De Havilland. Carl said they'll still be producing planes, but on a much smaller scale."

"Then why did you lose your job?"

"Because, now that there's enough men to take over, they don't need us women. We did men's jobs all through the war. But now that it's over, suddenly we're expendable."

"That's unfair," Myra said.

"You're telling me," I agreed. "But it's all the more reason to go back to school. If we get our diplomas, Myra, we'll be able to get higher-paying jobs. And my dad predicts there'll be boom years ahead. Just like after the last war."

"You're probably right. I'll talk to my mother again."

Chapter 34

Back To School

Myra's mother made her keep her job so I had to go back to Bloor Collegiate by myself.

It felt strange being in school again; I didn't know anybody in the fourth form. And after being a working woman for a whole year, it was hard to feel like a schoolgirl again.

I was only one year older than the other students in my home-form class—mostly girls because not many boys took shorthand and typing—but I felt much older and more mature.

The morning went by and I didn't speak to anybody. Oddly, I was shyer as a schoolgirl than I had been as a working girl.

Mother had packed my lunch: bologna sandwiches spread with mustard-pickle (her own recipe) and a yellow harvest apple from the tree in our backyard. I bought a ten-cent bottle of milk at the counter, and then I found myself a remote spot in the corner of the cafeteria. I intended to read another book from the library by James Hilton, presently my favourite author, but the noise in the cafeteria was so distracting. Boys were throwing orange peels at girls and the girls responded with squeals and shrieks of laughter. It was worse than eating in a factory.

My head started aching. I hadn't slept well the night before because I was worried about catching up. I shut my book and put my bread crusts in my lunch bag, a terrible habit that my dad deplored—wasting good food. "When I was a boy," he was famous for reiterating, "we were lucky to get enough to eat. We never wasted a crumb."

I scrunched up the bag and headed for the garbage can. Just as I lifted the lid, a tall girl with shoulder-length brown wavy hair (parted in the middle) and wearing a tunic, dropped her bag in first.

"Thanks," she said with a grin.

"You're welcome." I dropped my bag in and replaced the lid.

"I'm Alison Holt," she said as we left the noisy lunchroom and headed down the hall. "What's your name?"

"Ber—my name's Natalie Brigham." I nearly gave myself away.

"I don't remember seeing you last year. What form are you in?"

"Fourth form commercial," I said. "You didn't see me last year because I wasn't here. I was working."

"Where'd you work?"

"De Havilland. Making Mosquitoes—the fastest planes in the world."

"Sounds exciting," she said as we turned into room 207 and settled behind Underwood typewriters. "What made you decide to come back to school?"

"Oh, when the boys came back from the war, those who were lucky enough to come back all in one piece, they took our jobs and we girls were promptly fired."

"That's not fair."

"You're telling me."

The class filled up and the typing teacher, Miss Whitely, began dingling a little tea bell for attention.

"See you after," Alison said.

"Okay," I said. I liked her right away. She was pretty but not conceited. I could tell.

The second I placed my fingers on the home keys, I knew I was in trouble. The rest of the class began clacking away at about fifty miles an hour, or at least forty words a minute, and I was desperately picking and pecking trying to get the feel of the keys again.

By the end of typing period I was close to tears. Miss Whitely came down the aisle and stopped at my desk. "Can I help you?" she asked.

The kindness in her voice was my undoing. I tried to suppress the tears that filled my eyes. Luckily I had the eyelet hanky that Aunt Marie had given me in my blouse pocket.

"I've lost the touch," I said, dabbing my eyes. "I've missed a year and I'm way behind."

"Come back after school and we'll talk about it," she said.

I felt better after that and I surprised myself by doing okay in other subjects, such as shorthand and bookkeeping and English.

Alison waited for me in the hall while I went in to see Miss Whitely.

Miss Whitely's smile suited her name; her teeth were white as pearls and she had a dimple in one cheek.

In front of her, on her desk blotter, were my school records.

"I think the first thing we need to clear up is this," she said with an engaging smile. She was pointing with a pink fingernail to my name. *Beryl Brigham.*

"Yes, well..." I felt a bit foolish explaining. "When I went to get my registration card, so I could apply for war work, I decided to drop my real name and start all over again with a new name of my own choosing."

"You picked a nice one...Natalie," she smiled. "But what name is on your birth certificate?"

"Beryl," I admitted. "Beryl Jean Brigham."

"Well, that's your real name and always will be, but I'll call you Natalie. It suits you."

"Thank you, Miss Whitely." For a minute there I was afraid she was going to insist on Beryl.

"Now, then, let's get down to business. In order to earn your diploma, you'll need at least forty-five words a minute, sixty-five if you hope to achieve honours."

I gave a hopeless shrug. "I doubt if I can do it," I said.

"What you need is a typewriter at home to practice on. I presume you don't have one?"

"No. But I can get one. Maybe second-hand would do.

I've got war bonds I can cash."

"Good." Miss Whitely got her purse out of her desk drawer. "Get it as soon as possible. And don't worry, Natalie. Your speed will come back in no time with a little practice."

I walked down Dufferin Street with Alison. We told each other about our families.

"I've got three brothers," she said. "Danny and Bill and Ira."

"I've got just one younger brother…Rickey. He's cute but he's a nuisance."

"So, you had no brothers in the war," she said. I heard a catch in her voice and guessed what was coming. "Ira came home shell-shocked. He's still in the hospital, in the mental ward. Some days he knows us; some days he doesn't."

"I'm sorry," I said. "But I think I know how you feel. My cousin, Carmen—we're as close as brother and sister—is missing, presumed dead, but we haven't given up hope."

"I know."

Alison lived just two houses north of Aunt Marie's. "So long, see you tomorrow," I said. Then I decided to drop in on Aunt Marie.

I rang her doorbell for about three minutes but she didn't answer. I peered through the lace curtain on the little door window. I saw her cat, Mitzy, hunched in the kitchen doorway, obviously waiting for her. I rang again, waited a minute, then gave up and went home.

"How was school, Beryl?" My mother was so happy that I had agreed to go back.

"Okay," I said. "But I need a typewriter to practice on. I wonder if Eloise still has hers."

"Why don't you ask her after supper?" my mother said. "I've made your favourite tonight, lamb stew."

"Where did you get the meat coupons?" Some things were still rationed (meat was one) and our new books weren't due until the end of the week.

"Oh, I have my sources," Mom said with a conspiratorial laugh.

So after supper I went out the back door and through the space in the privet hedge to the Wilkinson's back door. I gave a pre-emptory knock and walked in.

Eloise was sitting in the corner, feeding Jamie a bottle. Her hair was a mess and the towel thrown over her shoulder was all splotched, but her face was glowing.

"Oh, look who's come to see you, Jamie!" she cried, turning the baby towards me without taking the bottle out of his mouth.

I leaned over and touched his bright pink cheek. "He sure is cute," I said.

Mrs. Wilkinson gave me a welcoming smile and Mr. Wilkinson looked up from his newspaper and nodded his head. Then Private James Foster came in from the dining room. He still looked a bit gaunt and he had a slight limp.

"Hi, Jim," I said. "How are you?"

"Okay," he said. He never said another word and he left the room moments later.

"Will you have a cup of tea with us, Beryl?" Mrs. Wilkinson said as she placed teacups around the oilcloth covered table.

"Sure," I said.

After he'd been burped successfully, Eloise took James the Third upstairs to bed. When she came back down she looked more like her old self. She had changed her dress and combed her hair and put a bit of lipstick on. "How's school, Beryl?" she asked, sitting beside me at the table.

"Why don't you ask Natalie," I said.

She laughed. "You are determined, aren't you?" she said.

"I am." I agreed. "And school is why I'm over here."

"Oh, and I thought you had come to see Jamie."

"That, too," I said. "But more specifically, I came to ask you if you still got your old Remington?"

"Yes, I have. Why do you ask?"

"Well, I'm rusty as an old nail and Miss Whitely—she's very nice—suggested that I practice typing at home. So I'll need a typewriter. Do you want to sell yours?"

"Oh, it's not worth much, Ber—Natalie. But you can borrow it for as long as you like. I don't know if I'll ever use it again." She gave a little sigh. "It will need a new ribbon, but otherwise I think it's in working order."

"I'll get it for you," Mr. Wilkinson said. "It's down the cellar." When he brought it up he said, "I'll carry it over for you, Beryl."

"Oh, no, I can manage," I said flexing my biceps. "War work builds muscles, you know."

Just before I went out the door, I turned to Eloise. "Let's go to the show some night soon," I said.

"That would be nice," she said. "I'll ask Jim what night would suit him."

As soon as she said that I knew we'd never go to the show together again. "Two's company, three's a crowd," I said laughingly as I went out the back door. Mr. Wilkinson shut the door behind me.

Chapter 35

Letter From Joan

Dear Dolores:

Today I got a letter from Joan. I was surprised because I hadn't heard from her in quite a while and I thought she had given up on our long-distance friendship. I thought maybe she had decided to get on with her life and that she might have a new boyfriend by now. In the picture she sent me of herself she looked cute and petite, the kind of girl most boys fall for. If you get my drift, Dolores. But, au contraire. She said she was tired of life without Carmen and she was thinking of coming to Canada. She asked me if it was easy to get a job here and would I ask around.

Well, Dolores, I had the funniest reaction to that idea. Did I really want another pretty girlfriend? The shortage of boys—I should say men—made the competition fierce, and all the war brides flowing across the ocean made it worse. It seemed like every soldier who came back either had a war bride on his arm or a girlfriend following after him.

I wouldn't talk like this to anyone else, Dolores,

because it sounds cheap and petty.

Well, school is going well and my typing speed is improving. And Carl asked me to the Halloween Dance at De Havilland. Alison is going to the Halloween Dance at the school, but the boys are all so young there. One of them, Peter O'Hearn, asked me to be his date at the dance. I said a polite no. He's cute but he looks like he hasn't had to shave yet. So I was glad when Carl called and I accepted with alacrity. It will be good to be back at De Havilland again.

Thanks for listening, Dolores.

> Yours,
> Natalie.

Nov. 2, 1945

Dear Dolores:

Well the Halloween Dance at De Havilland was a big disappointment. There were two girls there to every guy and Carl danced with all of them. I wasn't jealous, Dolores, honestly, because I'm not crazy about Carl. He's boring and full of himself.

But it's even more boring sitting at a table full of strangers (most of the gang I worked with had got fired or left), watching your date dance with every girl in sight. Next time Carl phones I'm going to say no. I've got a list of excuses ready.

I didn't answer Joan's last letter and today I got a

frantic one from her begging me to write. So I did. I told her I was too busy with my school work to be looking around for a job for her but I heard through the grapevine that jobs were plentiful if you had a skill.

Jim Foster is back in Christie Street Hospital. He needs an operation on his leg. They never did get the shrapnel out, so I guess they are going to try again. Eloise is worried sick. It's too bad because she had hoped they would be in their own flat by now. But it looks as if she'll have to stay with her parents a while longer. Not that they mind; they're crazy about their grandson.

I have to go now, Dolores; I have ten pages of typing to do (my speed is increasing every day) and I also have to make carbon copies. I hate that because the carbon paper makes me nervous and I make mistakes, and when I try to rub out the mistake on the carbon copy, it smears.

Yours truly,
Natalie.

Chapter 36

The Registered Letter

I left the house in a hurry. I'd slept in and didn't want to be late for school. Miss Whitely had been so nice to me, and I needed all the help I could get if I was going to pass fourth form. I tripped on the porch stairs and lost my shoes. I had to turn around to retrieve them. I jammed my feet into the toes of my loafers and flip-flopped my way to the sidewalk.

The chill of fall was upon us, and winter was just around the corner. The last of the leaves on the tops of the trees were swirling to the ground where they were caught in little eddies. I pulled my cardigan closer and hugged my waist. I trudged on with my head bowed. The school year stretched out interminably ahead of me, and I sighed as I thought of the challenges ahead. But I was resigned to it. Mom was right. I needed an education to get a decent job, especially now that the men were back and given jobs before any of us girls—women—could be hired. I sighed. The world of work and war had changed me. I felt almost old now, especially sitting in class beside all those giggly girls who were one whole year younger than I was.

I spied a white birch, now nearly naked, and thought of

how the Indians wrote on the bark many moons ago. One golden leaf zigzagged through the air like a little canoe on a current, and the sweet smell of the crunching leaves wafting up my nose, gave me a melancholy feeling. I stopped to take a deep, delicious breath of the cool air.

Suddenly a scream pierced the quiet and jolted me out of my reverie. It came from my Aunt Marie's house, the same awful scream that had sailed down the street the day she got the letter saying Carmen was presumed dead. What could it be now? Had she received his dog tags? I stood transfixed on the sidewalk in front of her house.

The grey silhouette of my aunt behind the screen door, her hand holding a letter in front of her face, was still as a statue. With a little whimper she unfroze and her arm sunk slowly to her side. Immediately school was banished from my mind.

"Aunt Marie," I called, running right out of my shoes up to her door. "What's wrong?" I opened the screen and she held an official looking envelope out to me by the corner, like something contaminated.

"I don't know. It's from them."

I saw the words, "Department of National Defence" in the corner of the brown envelope and "confidential" stamped in blood red letters across it.

"Well, gosh, open it. Quick. Let's see what it says."

"I can't." Her terrified eyes met mine.

"It might be good news." I tried in a faltering voice.

"Oh mercy me." She began pacing in agitated little steps. She turned beseechingly to me. "You look."

I snatched the letter from her quivering hand and tore it open.

Dear Mrs. Baker:

It is with great pleasure we inform you that your son, Sergeant Carmen Alan Baker, RCAF squadron 677, has been returned to us in a prisoner exchange, and will be arriving in Halifax aboard HMS Louis Pasteur, estimated time 1400 hours on December first, where he will be taken to Camp Hill Military Hospital...

"He's alive! Aunt Marie, oh my gosh, he's alive!"

"He's alive," she repeated and a weird smile flickered across her face, eyes still haunted with disbelief.

"He's alive," we whispered together.

Chapter 37

POW

The letter informed us gravely that Carmen had been interned in a German prisoner of war camp, Stalag Luft 1. Through some mix up, the Canadian Armed Forces had not been informed of his whereabouts. He had broken his ankles and some bones in his feet when he had jumped from his plane and parachuted behind enemy lines. He was the only member of his crew to survive. His broken feet would have to be reset at the military hospital in downtown Halifax. He would not be strong enough to make the trip home for three to four weeks.

I flew home to tell Mom, with Aunt Marie trying to keep up.

"Mom, Mom! Guess what?" I screeched. I stood huffing and puffing in the front hallway.

"Beryl, why aren't you—" she stopped short at the sight of me. Then she noticed Aunt Marie, who was standing on the front porch, wringing her hands. She opened the door and helped her in, then turned to me in wide-eyed wonder,

"Whatever is the matter?" she implored.

"He's alive, Mom. Carmen!" Only then did the full realization hit me and I started to sob.

"Oh, Mom. He's not dead."

"Praise God. Oh, I always felt that he was. Oh, thank the Lord."

Aunt Marie looked in amazement from Mom to me, still trying to grasp the miracle that had befallen her in the last fifteen minutes. Then we grabbed her to us in a hug, and all three of us jumped up and down in unison, laughing and crying at the same time.

It was decided then and there that I would go with Aunt Marie to Halifax. She seemed a bit better with the news, but was still quite befuddled and needed a companion on the long overnight train trip. Mom wrote a letter to Miss Whitely, who showed it to the principal. Given the special nature of the circumstances, I was allowed two days off school (plus the weekend) for the trek—my very first visit to the East Coast, and the longest trip of my entire life so far.

Chapter 38

The Trip

It was my first time inside Union Station on Front Street. I was instantly overwhelmed. I bumped into people, buzzing about like bees in a hive, as I gazed up at the cathedral ceiling. I was awestruck. For the first time I saw my city as a tourist would, and I was filled with pride. Toronto, the capital of Ontario, the biggest city in Canada. I forged a path to the boarding gate, excusing us all the way, with Aunt Marie in tow. She didn't seem nervous; she didn't seem anything. She just stared blankly at all the commotion and trustingly followed my lead. I'm glad she didn't know how scared I was inside. Sometimes I didn't feel all grownup despite my war work. I hoped I wasn't regressing to my former self, a high-schoolgirl again.

Soon after we settled into our sleeping car, the train rumbled to a start. It wound its way by the backs of grubby buildings (a side of Toronto that I hoped the tourists wouldn't see), then by long skinny backyards lined up like sardines along the tracks. A stout woman wearing an apron paused from hanging her wash on the line to wave at us. I waved back and smiled, but I don't think she saw me. Then, out the window, all was a blur of bushes and far-off trees as far as the eye could see. I thought I spotted Lake Ontario on the horizon, but maybe it was a mirage. (Actually, I think it was on the other side.) Aunt Marie was mesmerized, perched with folded hands on the seat beside me, her nose an inch from the glass. A hunger pain stabbed my stomach, so I opened the lunch mom had packed. I offered an egg salad and cucumber sandwich to Aunt Marie. She stuck her hand out without as much as a glance and kept looking at the fuzzy scene. What was she thinking? I tried to fathom. It was then that I started to ponder what we would find in Halifax. What would Carmen look like? I shuddered. I pictured him plummeting to the earth, dangling at the end of a parachute and landing with a crunch of bones on the ground. I winced. His time as a POW I couldn't begin to imagine. Why hadn't he communicated with us himself when he arrived back in England? Fear welled up inside me and I looked with trepidation at Aunt Marie, her fragile frame joggling along beside me with faraway eyes. She was too tired to resist anymore, as she passively awaited what fate would present her next.

In Halifax we were swept along with the swarm of passengers, out of the station and into the bright sunlight, where taxis lined up like a trail of black ants homeward bound. A car door flew open and we were engulfed by the back seat of a cab. The musty smell of old cigar smoke caught in my throat and I coughed as I handed the driver a piece of paper with the address of The Lord Nelson Hotel carefully printed on it.

I peered out the window at the stately trees and ornate homes painted bright blue, yellow and green, even pink. White gingerbread trim decorated high-peaked roofs on gables. I could hardly contain my excitement as my head bobbed from side, to side taking in the gorgeous view.

"Look, Aunt Marie. How beautiful it is!"

Her eyes brightened as she peered at the lovely scene whizzing by. I had always imagined Halifax to be a dreary place, nothing but smoke stacks and factories and shipyards, and even blocks of rubble, flattened buildings leftover from the Halifax explosion during the First World War, which I'd learned about in school. It just goes to show what an education travel is, I marvelled. Then and there, I vowed to discover the real places my history classes had introduced me to. My earlier fears of the day vanished as the travel bug took hold of me. I saw myself in the future, Natalie Brigham—a citizen of the world.

Suddenly the cabby did a U-turn and we jerked to a halt in front of the most regal building I had ever seen. I sighed with satisfaction. It was well worth it to spend my war bonds feeling like a queen. A uniformed man left his post to rush down to open the cab door for us and we mounted the steps. The doorman in black uniform with red piping opened the tall door inlaid with pure gold! For a split second I wondered if the Governor General himself was waiting to greet us in the lobby. The Queen's guard took our tapestry luggage and ushered us through the door.

My eyes took a moment to adjust, and gradually a majestic scene appeared. Fine ladies and gentlemen milled about the red velvet carpet. Some sat demurely chatting on loveseats or reading in plush wing chairs in golden pools of light, cast by brass lamps sitting on heavy oak tables. Our Sunday best felt instantly shabby amidst all this finery. The doorman was gone and we were on our own to negotiate our way to the front desk, formal and intimidating. I suddenly felt woozy. The excitement of the day had taken its toll on me. I was really far from home. (One thousand miles, in fact!) A twinge of homesickness tugged at my throat. I missed my mom. My heart sank like a stone and all I wanted was a bed to lie down on.

Chapter 39

The Hospital

I awoke with a start with dim light forming a line down the middle of the drapes. The clock on the bedside table said 6:30. I didn't move so as not to wake Aunt Marie. I wondered if she had brought her smelling salts with her in case she had one of her spells.

We were both completely done in and had gone to bed as soon as we got to our room the night before. We'd pulled our nighties from our bags without unpacking so much as our toothbrushes. I'd yanked back the heavy spread and we'd slid down inside the tight, white sheets beside each other and had gone to sleep without saying a word. To my surprise, I'd slept like a log.

When I opened my eyes, I didn't know where I was, but it soon dawned on me. I stared at the swirly plaster ceiling. A queasy feeling filled my stomach and I swallowed hard to muster my courage as I pondered the day ahead. Excitement tinged with dread buzzed in my brain. There was so much we didn't know. How would he look? What should we say? Should we ask him about it? Some soldiers didn't want to talk about their experiences in the camps ever again. A veil would fall over their eyes like a shroud, and they'd shuffle away without uttering a word at the mere mention of the war. Alison said her brother still hadn't stopped shaking. There was nothing to do but play it by ear. I stretched and turned to Aunt Marie. Her eyes were wide open; she too had been contemplating the ceiling.

"You're awake."

"Um-hum."

"Are you ready to get up?"

"Um-hum."

"I'm starved. Are you ready for breakfast?"

"Uh-uh."

"It's probably too early anyway, but we could order some tea from room service. That would be fun, wouldn't it?"

"Yes, that would be nice." That was the most normal response I'd heard from her in ages. I felt immediately heartened, jumped to my feet and pattered across the spongy carpet to the bathroom. I started sloshing in the washbasin and ran my tongue over my teeth. Eww. They were all mossy. I rustled in my overnight kit for my toothbrush. I could see Aunt Marie in the mirror. She was up, fishing her stockings out of the jumble in her suitcase, stretching them like elastic bands and muttering to herself. We were on our way to the hospital within the hour.

The nurse on duty looked startled to see visitors so early. When we said how far we'd come and whom we'd come to see, she softened a bit and padded off on thick-soled white shoes, her wide posterior protruding like a shelf under her uniform, starched stiff as a tent. She disappeared with a swish behind a door with an opaque window. I ran and stuck my nose on the glass, squinting with all my might, but I couldn't see so much as a shadow. I put my eye against the door crack. Nothing.

"Beryl, you get away from there, for the love of Pete!"

Her reprimand made me laugh and relief flooded over me. I was no longer alone on this mission. My motherly aunt had been restored to me.

The nurse returned, and with a curt nod said, "You may go in. He's in the last bed on the right. You have fifteen minutes. Not a moment longer."

I paused at the door and gulped. My eyes were stinging and threatening to betray me, and my legs wobbled.

"Well?" said Aunt Marie indignantly. "What are we waiting for?"

I swung the heavy door open and we stepped into the ward. Two rows of iron beds lined either wall. Pails and tubes and medical contraptions hung above and below every bed. An acrid antiseptic smell assailed my nostrils and I sneezed. Tousled heads turned in our direction, then lifted off the pillows, straining to see the early visitors huddled in the doorway. I smiled sidelong at the peaked faces, afraid of what I might see as I passed. I followed my brazen aunt stalwartly down the aisle, who waved querulous nurses from her path saying breathlessly, "Where's my boy?" She stopped short and I bumped into her.

There he was.

Sitting on the end of his bed with his crutches by his side, Carmen looked for all the world like the father he'd never known. His shoulders were slumped and his chest sunken. If I'd seen him on a crackly, black and white newsreel, I'd never have recognized him. But when he saw us, he straightened up and took a deep breath, which filled his frail frame with life. His mouth dropped open without a sound. I broke into a run and threw my arms around him in a torrent of emotion. As soon as I felt his bony body, I eased my grip and hugged him gingerly. I let go to wipe my tears and turned to my trembling aunt.

"Oh Car—" she croaked, and when she held his upturned face in both of her hands, the boy's eyes returned to the man's face.

"Oh, Ma, I'm home." He dropped his head to hide his tears and we buried him with our embrace, fervently stroking his head and patting his back.

The nurse who'd been looking on misty-eyed let out a huge "Tut" of disapproval and dove to save him from being smothered.

"That's enough for now, I'd say. We have to get him ready for surgery."

"Surgery?" my aunt exclaimed.

"Yes, to reset his feet and ankles. You'll have to run along now and come back tomorrow."

"It's nothing Ma, really. The doctor said I'll be as good as new. I probably won't even have a limp in time."

Aunt Marie planted herself in front of him, wringing her hands, waiting for more reassurance, but the nurse took her elbow and steered her away.

"Don't you worry about a thing, Mrs. Baker. We'll take good care of him."

We backed our way down the aisle, waving feebly as Carmen smiled with amusement at us, as though he hadn't a worry in the world.

Chapter 40

My Fate

The rest of the day crawled by at a snail's pace. Aunt Marie had no interest in sightseeing so we spent it pacing, poking at our meals, and repeating how well he looked to reassure our failing spirits. Finally we fell silent on either end of a loveseat in the hotel lobby which had become ordinary overnight.

I felt the urge to write to Dolores. I swear she had become real to me! I even knew what she looked like. A pang of guilt welled up inside me. I thought of my curt reply to Joan's last letter. I couldn't write to my imaginary friend as long as Joan sat pining across the sea, waiting for more news from me. I'd have to tell Carmen about our correspondence, and she'd have to know that he was safe and sound. Why was I so possessive of him?

Myra had got a letter from her soldier friend, but I hadn't heard a single word from Reggie. I got a glowing letter from Rachel saying she'd married an English airforceman! "Darn, maybe I should have joined up," I lamented then. I'd found out via the grapevine that Will had married an English girl named Lois because I hadn't promised to wait for him. "Who needs him anyway? I never would have looked twice at him in peacetime," I'd retorted indignantly. But then a lump filled my throat remembering the day that Dad looked up from his newspaper and our eyes met. He didn't have to speak. He just folded the paper and handed it to me.

"Who is it, Dad?" I whispered as I took it. He pointed to the column. I ran my finger down it and stopped halfway. There was Will's name. Killed in action.

I shook the memory from my mind. I was done with being sad. Deep down I knew that I had a future much different from my friends'. I finally realized what I wanted to do with my life. I would become a teacher—a history teacher, so the past would not be forgotten. I wanted the young to know how awful it was for all of us, not only for the boys who went away—James and Reggie and Will and Alison's brother, Ira—but also for the girls they'd left behind. It must never, never happen again! There must be no more war. Not another Dieppe, where 900 Canadians lost their lives and 2000 went missing. No more corpses floating in the shallow water, bloated and nameless as dead fish. Maybe one day I would meet a man with a mission, like me, and we'd get married and have babies and live to a ripe old age, as those boys never would, but always remembering what they did for us thousands of miles from home, defending our freedom.

Chapter 41

Carmen's Big News

The nurse wasn't at the front desk when we arrived at the hospital, and we didn't wait around. Aunt Marie pushed the door open and we fairly ran down the aisle. We could see Carmen's ungainly position instantly. On his back, his swaddled legs were spread akimbo, suspended in mid-air. He was propping himself up on both elbows, trying to find a comfortable position.

"Ladies, ladies, hold your horses. You have to sign in!" an indignant nurse cried after us.

"Oh, my stars. What have you done to him?" Aunt Marie hollered back at her. She stopped at his bedside, panting, staring in amazement at his legs and feet held up by pulleys. She began nervously fussing with his sheets, which were all askew, while I stood gaping at the sight.

Carmen let himself fall back on his pillow.

"It looks worse than it is. I'm okay, Ma. They gave me a shot and I'm feeling no pain," he said with a goofy smile, wobbling his head. Then he turned to the disgruntled nurse who hovered at the foot of his bed.

"Could I have some breakfast?"

"I'll go check with the doctor on duty." Possessive of her patient, she pushed by us to plump up his pillow, then strode away.

His chipper tone was reassuring, so we settled ourselves on two chairs beside his bed. It was then I remembered. I opened my bag and pulled his blue airforce cap out and presented it to him triumphantly.

"You've still got it!" he cried gleefully.

"It hung on the back of my closet door, waiting for you to come home." I didn't mention that I had removed it and put it away in despair. I placed it on his head and it looked ridiculous with his hospital gown. We all laughed at the sight, even the young, toothless man grinning at us from the next bed.

Aunt Marie began, "We were told you were missing in action and then presumed dead!" She choked up and couldn't go on.

"I didn't even know who I was at first. My dog tags were lost. I couldn't remember a thing after the jump. When I woke up, I was in an infirmary and the doctors and nurses were speaking German! I was told I had shell shock syndrome—amnesia. It wasn't until they transported me across the channel to a hospital for servicemen in Bournemouth, England, that it all came back to me."

He had to rest a moment then went on when he got his breath. His eyes began to shine.

"There was the loveliest nurse. She had blue, blue eyes like yours." He looked straight into mine. "Her name was Beryl!"

I caught my breath at the sound of my forsaken name.

"Then, for sure I knew I wasn't 'John Smith.' As nurse Beryl continued to talk to me I started to remember, bit by bit. When she told me her name, I got a clear picture of a girl I'd left behind, my cousin and best friend, Beryl, and I knew I had to get better. After that I'd wake up from my dreams with other people in my mind—first you, Mom— and their names would pop out of my mouth."

We stared in wonder at the tale; it just kept getting more and more amazing. Life truly is stranger than fiction, I thought.

"It was a girl named Beryl who brought me back to the land of the living. My life came together like the pieces of a jigsaw puzzle. Everything came clear. I realized something else, Mom…. There's something important I wanted to tell you face to face." He looked at his mother, who braced herself for more incredible news.

"There's another girl, a wonderful woman I met at Hendon airbase. Her name is Joan."

I blinked at the sound of the name and wondered what was coming.

"I want to marry her, if she'll still have me," he said firmly.

"Good Lord. What next?" my aunt protested. "You're too young to marry. You're only nineteen!"

Now that Carmen was really back, she reverted to being her old self, an overprotective mother. He would always be her baby.

Carmen eased himself onto his side, groaning a little with the effort, and looked directly into her eyes.

"If I'm old enough to go to war, Ma—to nearly die for my country—I'm old enough to know what I want," he said bluntly.

"I don't know…I suppose," she wondered aloud as she deflated in her chair, heaving an exhausted sigh.

I had to confess. "Joan and I have been writing. She wants to come to Canada. I know she'll say yes; she'll marry you."

"Really? Great!" he exclaimed.

"You three have cooked this up behind my back," Aunt Marie accused indignantly.

"No. I showed you the letters. Don't you remember?" I protested weakly. She looked bemused for a moment, searching her mind, sifting through the fog of the last months.

The nurse arrived with a tray and cut in. "Here's your breakfast. Two coddled eggs and dry toast. Let's see how that goes down."

She turned her gloating gaze on us. "You will have to go and let him eat in peace," she said with authority.

Aunt Marie didn't protest, but immediately gathered herself together and placed a kiss on her son's forehead.

Then he looked beseechingly to me, hoping for an ally. "Beryl? Will you write a letter for me to Joan? My hands are still a little shaky."

"Sure. I'll bring some hotel stationary tomorrow and you can dictate it." Then I added, "I'd love to."

Chapter 42

Dear Joan

Carmen was intent on writing the letter as soon as we arrived the next day. Aunt Marie decided she needed a cup of tea and a bite to eat, so she went to the hospital cafeteria. We were alone at last.

"Are you sure about this, Carm?" I implored.

"Oh, Beryl. I'm in love with Joan. Believe me, I'm not the same kid who went away. War changes a person."

"Oh, I know, I know."

I pulled a writing pad out of my purse and poised my pen.

Dear Joan, I began. "Okay. What do you want me to write?"

"I thought you'd know what to say," he said sheepishly.

"Oh no. Nothing doing. Now just think about it and say it plain and simple. Start with what happened since you last saw each other and go from there."

It took about an hour to write a page with him awkwardly trying to put his feelings into words (with some help from me). Then I addressed the envelope to Joan Summerville, 120 Victoria Street, Hendon, England. My heart fluttered as I looked at my girlish writing, knowing the joy this surprise letter from Carmen would bring to Joan, and I felt good all over. Then we started to talk like we used to when we strolled down Yonge Street arm-in-arm before the war.

"I'd really like it if you'd take Joan around and be her friend," he said.

"I'm already her friend," I replied, and in that moment I knew I meant it.

"I was hoping you'd sort of Canadianize her."

Instantly I was hopping mad. This happened all the time. Our boys would come home with war brides and want them to "act Canadian" overnight. If they wanted Canadian wives, why didn't they come back and marry the girls they'd left behind? I hid my annoyance as best I could.

"I won't try to change her, if that's what you mean. I like her the way she is, and so should you." I'd got to know Joan from our correspondence in spite of myself. Now I spoke with true fondness of this adoring girl, who I had to admit, loved him as much or more than I did.

"Oh, I do, I do!" he protested.

"She'll always be British deep down, but gradually she'll become Canadian like all immigrants do. I wouldn't want her to lose her heritage. It'll be great fun having an English girlfriend!"

"Yes, yes, you're right," he blurted, looking a little ashamed of his request.

Aunt Marie came back. She took the thin hand of her only son, so miraculously restored to her, and gazed intently into his face with a gratitude I'd never seen before.

"All I care about is that you are safe and sound. The only thing I want is for you to be happy. If you love this girl, then I know I'll love her too."

Carmen put his arm around his mother's neck and pulled her to him. I tried to slip away discretely, saying I needed a cup of tea, but Carmen looked up.

"Beryl."

"Yes?"

"Thanks Beryl...for everything."

"Heck. What's a second cousin once removed for?"

As I walked through the winding hospital corridors, I heard the sound of my name, as Carmen had said it, over and over in my mind. My real name, Beryl, was as welcome to me now as the call of a long, lost friend. I knew then that Natalie was a borrowed identity, tried on by a girl living in difficult times. War makes a person grow up. Natalie was a whimsical girl. Beryl was a woman, ready to live life to the fullest in a new time, a booming post-war world that would need strong, capable men and women, like Carmen and me.

Afterword

My mother, Bernice Thurman Hunter, died on May 29, 2002. One month before she died, she asked me, "If any-thing happens to me, will you finish my book?" Sadly, that is what occurred.

Mom often reminisced with her family about wartime. We indulged her as she repeated vivid memories, which still pained her fifty years later. She would stare into space and say wistfully, "I went with my cousin Grant to the show to see *My Friend Flicka* the night before he went away. He was only eighteen." Then she would draw a long sigh and finish, "He never came back. His plane was shot down two weeks before the war ended." So in her story she righted that terri-ble wrong. In Mom's stories justice prevails.

With trepidation I began my task, sifting through copious, hand-scrawled notes, looking for clues to how she intended to end the book. I found the gold nugget I needed, written on a tiny yellow Post-it Note. Three words: *Carmen comes home.*

Each time I sat down to write, one of Mom's anecdotes would pop into my mind just when I needed it—her words, her voice, indelible in my memory. It became a surprisingly effortless labour of love, my last gift to her—the completion of her last book. It was her tribute to all the "girls and boys" of war and a treasure for all of us who are left behind.

Heather Anne Hunter